HOW MY BROTHER'S BEST FRIEND STOLE CHRISTMAS

MOLLY O'KEEFE

LETTER TO READERS

Hey everyone! Happiest of Holidays to all of you. I hope How My Brother's Best Friend Stole Christmas is the shot of sexy holiday spirit you need! This is the third book in the Kane Co Series - but can totally be read as a standalone! If you're interested in the other two books in the series - one-click here!

My Fake Christmas Fiancé by Julie Kriss

Santa Baby Maybe by S. Doyle

If you're looking for more Christmas romance (though not as spicy as HMBBFSC) check out Christmas At The Riverview Inn!

UNTITLED

Kane Family Christmas

1

———

S ophie

YOU KNOW WHAT'S BULLSHIT? Those scenes in movies when a girl gets all dressed up. And she's got on high heels and makeup, and a tight dress that shows off the ass and boobs she's been pretending she doesn't have because she doesn't know what to do with them. Then, with the ass and boobs on full display, she walks into a big fancy party, and the guy she's been secretly pining for most of her life sees her and instantly falls in love.

Like fake eyelashes and a push-up bra were what he needed to finally see her for the total fox she'd always been.

Total bullshit, right?

Well, guess who was putting on a push-up bra and a pair of high heels that were probably going to break her ankle.

Yeah. Me.

This was what fifteen years of Sam Porter in my life had reduced me to: a Christmas Eve makeover.

I was officially *that girl.*

My phone buzzed on the edge of the desk, but I ignored it. I could really only do one thing at a time right now. And all my energy was on this—my mental breakdown.

"Okay," my friend Joy said. "It's time to go look in a mirror."

"Can't I just take your word for it?"

"Well, you haven't yet."

She marched me from my desk in the big main room of the Kane Co warehouse down the small hallway to the employee break room, which had a mirror for making sure there wasn't food in your teeth after lunch.

Joy was all zen and easy because Joy was all zen and easy. And she was glamorous in a low-key way that made me believe she knew what to do with eyeliner and a curling iron. Until I found out she was about as clueless as I was and she just got lucky with all that low-key glamour, which probably came with the gig of being an artist. Joy was the head glass artist at Kane Co.

We make holiday ornaments. Well, she does. I ship them.

You know what kind of glamour comes with the gig of warehouse supervisor? None.

So...makeover.

Joy was a dream with the hair and makeup but as clueless as me when it came to the dress and the shoes, so we'd gone shopping a week ago and gotten professional help. Shopping was not at all my thing, but Joy got me a bubble tea every time I wanted to bolt from the mall. It was an expensive, fattening day. But we got the job done and I bought a dress of blue sequins that made me feel like a beautiful disco ball. Joy got a dress too. She had a whole embarrassed thing with her boobs, which were amazing, but tonight the two of us were ignoring our mother's voices in our heads and years of not knowing what to do with ourselves and we were going *all out*.

Joy was wearing a strapless black cocktail dress that made her look like a Bond Girl.

"Shoes," she said, pushing a pair of strappy, glittery high heels in front of me.

In for a penny and all that shit. I put the shoes on, and because I couldn't bend over in my dress without popping the seam over my ass, I let Joy buckle the shoes.

She stood up and put her hands on my shoulders. She was trying hard not to smile.

"Are you laughing at me?" I gasped, shocked she would do that, but she wasn't the first and totally wouldn't be the last.

"No, no, honey. Never. I'm smiling because you look..."

"Ridiculous?" I put a hand to my hair, which was like an explosion of corkscrew curls over my shoulder held in place with glittery barrettes. This was why I wore ponytails and ball caps, because my hair was the worst and Joy had spent, like, an *hour* on it.

"No. Honey. Look..."

She stepped to the side and turned me around to face the break room mirror. And the person looking back at me was...

"Holy shit," I breathed, stepping forward to look closer in the mirror. "That's me."

I'd worn the dress at the mall. The shoes. But the whole package was something...else.

Those were my eyes. My terrible hair made into some-thing...fun. I wore a tight blue sequined dress that was held up by a strap on one shoulder, and my arms, strong and toned from my work in the company, looked pretty damn good. Freckles and all. My nonexistent boobs had been given an existence and my ass...I mean *my ass.* "Look at my ass!"

"Total knockout," she said. "But let's..." She stepped in behind me and then reached out and pushed my lips up into a smile. "There. Now. You are a total fucking knockout."

If I'd been the kind of twenty-five-year-old who giggled, I would have giggled. That's how good I looked. How good I felt. Which I had not expected to come from this makeover.

"We're pretty hot, Joy," I said, pulling us together, side by side, to look at ourselves in the mirror. The Bond Girl and the Disco Ball.

"I wasn't sure about this, but I have to agree. We are pretty hot," she said.

Joy reached up and did a scrunchy type thing she'd been doing for two hours to my hair. Like there was any chance my hair was going to lose the curl. I'd been praying for my hair to lose its curl since I was a kid, and no dice.

She'd covered my lips in bright red lipstick. My eyes in glittery eye shadow. I was me but...sexier. Brighter.

I had not expected miracles here, but it sort of felt like one had happened.

"He doesn't stand a chance," Joy said to my reflection.

I'd said not one word about Fucking Sam Porter. Not one. But Joy knew. Hell, maybe everyone knew. Butterflies exploded in my stomach.

"Am I that obvious?" I couldn't keep the panic out of my voice. I mean, if I walked into that party and people knew what I was after...forget it. I'd put my jeans back on and drop this stupid idea.

"No. But I have a sense about these things," she said. "As

long as I've been here, you haven't been interested in shopping or makeup or hair products, and suddenly your brother's best friend shows up and you're..." She waved her hands around me.

I groaned and put my head in my hand. All this time, I'd thought I was playing it so cool. "You want to talk about it?" Joy asked.

"God no," I said. Talk about Sam? How? Like, what words would I even use? If there were words to describe him and how I felt...well, I didn't know them. I didn't know the language.

Joy laughed. "If you change your mind, I'm here."

Joy was the big-deal ornament designer my brother had hired to turn Kane Co. Inc around. Prong one of his three-pronged approach to saving our family business. Joy was half witch, half artist, half...absolute goofball. And yeah, yeah, that was three halves.

I stood there in the shipping break room in a sequined gown and high-heeled shoes (that weirdly didn't hurt my feet) among the beat-up lockers and the old fridge and the bulletin board with the Heimlich and CPR posters and the sign-up sheet to buy popcorn from Rodrigo's kid's Boy Scout troop.

So, yeah, I looked like a fish out of water in this place I'd created and controlled. Where I felt strong and capable and the lingering shit from my parents couldn't touch me.

But up there. Up on the top floor with the new windows and the big deck and all the staff and everyone in suits and dresses and my mom floating around like some kind of poisonous cloud...ugh.

This was a mistake. I could feel it in my bones. I wasn't some woman in a rom-com whose life got wrapped up in a bow in an hour and a half.

I was Sophie Kane, the black sheep of the Kane family. The embarrassing one. The screwup. And I just looked stupid in this dress.

"Stop!" Joy cried. Because she was part witch, she could tell I was about to tear the thing off my body. "Stop. You look beautiful. You do. And I won't fight you if you want to go out there in your jeans and hoodie. You're beautiful that way, too. But that dress cost so much money."

It really had. Come to find out, sequins were expensive.

"Fine," I snapped. "Let's just...do this."

I'd spent most of my life wearing smooth the grooves between embarrassment and anger. I'd made that a real easy transition for myself. I could go from embarrassed to outrage in .05 seconds. I wasn't proud of it, but whatever. When you grew up with my mom you learned some fucked-up coping mechanisms. I mean, look at my brother. The shit that guy did? That bravado? Getting engaged to some strange woman on a whim? It wasn't healthy.

Joy handed me a little black purse. "What do I need that for?" I asked.

"Lipstick. Key badge. Phone. Condoms?"

I felt myself blush bright red. So fast and so hard I got dizzy.

"Isn't that the point of all of this beauty?" she asked. Waving a finger over all her hard work. "To get laid?"

Was that what I wanted from Fucking Sam Porter? To get laid? I mean, the truth was that I had imagined it more times than I could count. But my imagination and reality were miles apart. Sam talked to me all the time–about the Broncos and Skyrim. Books we were reading. Some politics. My brother, Wes, and how he had lost his mind with this crazy engagement.

So, what I wanted...really, really wanted was for Sam to

look at me with...I don't know, softness? Care? Not see me as one of the guys, but as...me?

Not my brother's little sister.

Not the pesky kid who'd followed him around all those years.

Not the trash-talking video game buddy.

I wanted Sam Porter to see *me*.

The girl who'd loved him silently but passionately for five long years.

"Fine," I grabbed the purse. "The condoms are in there?"

"Three," Joy said with a waggle of her eyebrows. "Just in case."

All of this felt stupid. Stupid, stupid. But I was doing it. I had a thong on, so there was no point in backing out now. "Let's go," I said and we left the break room to go back to the main room of the warehouse with my desk and the packing section and the shelves of ornaments.

Joy grabbed her own purse. Another tiny little bag, but whatever she saw in there made her face go white. Her entire body still.

"You okay?" I asked.

"Fine," she said, closing the bag and waving me off. "Just something I forgot. Let's go."

I picked up my phone from where it had been sitting facedown for the duration of this makeover. I had two missed calls from my brother and a bunch of texts.

Hey! The first one said. *Are you at the party? I can't find you.*

Soph, the second one said. *Get up here now! I'm making an announcement...*

Crap, said the third. *I can't put this off any longer. Hurry your ass up.*

Well, shit, I thought. This seemed dramatic. But then, everything with my brother was dramatic these days.

The shipping department was on the first floor of the Kane Co. building, separated by a door from the workshops where Joy made her magical you-wouldn't-freaking-believe-how-expensive-they-are Christmas ornaments. The workshop had windows that allowed people to stroll by on the sidewalk, look in, and get swept up in Joy and her crew of glassblowers.

I had a heart made out of concrete and zero Christmas spirit, and even I was amazed by what they could do.

The party was on the top floor. The fancy floor. You can probably guess how much time I spent there.

Zero. The answer is zero.

My brother had gone all out for this party. And let me tell you, usually Christmas was a dry, panicked affair around here. Like, we spent all this time creating wonder and good cheer only to ship it off and leave ourselves with none. But since Dad was arrested and Wes took over, Kane Co. was turning things around. A few weeks ago I almost put up a tree in my own apartment. Almost.

We climbed the three steps out of the warehouse, through the door into the cool and quiet workshop to the lobby.

The elevators were doing a brisk business shuttling employees and guests up to the fifth floor. Outside snow was swirling. Another winter storm that was about to pound Denver. But what bothered the good citizens of Denver every other day was somehow magical on Christmas Eve. Everyone coming in laughed, red cheeked, as they shrugged snow off their coats and brushed it out of their hair.

Standing there, surrounded by holiday joy and delight, dressed like some kind of holiday vixen, I allowed myself to get swept up in the spirit—in the possibility. And I let go of my fear and my stress and I let myself to believe that everything was going to be all right.

That this holiday party was going to be the start of a whole new life for Kane Co., for my brother, but especially for me.

And Fucking Sam Porter.

2

———

Once we got up to the party, Joy took off like a shot. And I realized how much I'd been counting on her as a wingman.

Okay. All right. No need to panic.

I needed to find my Drama Queen brother anyway.

The party floor was amazing. There was a band and free-flowing booze and waiters walking around with snacks on trays, all making it clear that just because my father had been hauled off for embezzlement no one needed to panic. There was a new sheriff in town—that sheriff being my brother—and things were A-okay at Kane Co.

The band was a nice touch.

I skirted the edge of the party, where the shadows were thick. People were gathered around cocktail tables talking shit and eating fancy snacks. They were laughing—which was good—and I slipped by them all, unnoticed or maybe even unrecognized by employees.

Getting cocky I grabbed a glass of champagne from a passing waiter and turned, only to come face to face with my mother. Gloria Kane.

Oh God.

"I didn't recognize you," she said. My mother was the personification of a cool breeze. A draft that made you reach for a blanket. She wore a black suit; she always wore a black suit. Her only nod to the holiday was a pin on the jacket, a gold circle that maybe was supposed to be a wreath. I mean, ho-ho-ho and all that. Her hair was in its bun, pulled so tight it made my own head hurt.

"It's a party," I said, running a hand across the navy sequins of my dress.

"I thought I'd dress up."

"You look lovely," she said. And leaned in for one of those two cheek air kisses. I was so stunned by the compliment I gave the air around her cheeks kisses of my own. But nothing came free from Gloria Kane, especially compliments. "It really is too bad you inherited your father's hair. You always look like you've rolled in hay." She pulled a curl straight, until it stung my scalp and I pushed her hand away.

She turned, looking out at the party and the fancy decorations, and I resisted the urge to rub away the sting of my scalp. The room was beautiful. The silver tinsel and the bright red and green baubles, the lights and beauty, and it looked *expensive*. It was so different from the way it had been when my father ran things. "You've heard, I suppose. He probably told you. You were probably there," Mom said.

"Where?"

"At the wedding."

Mom looked over at me and I couldn't handle my shock. My surprise. Or...maybe my hurt. "Penny and Wes? They... did it?" I asked.

"Apparently."

"Bullshit." *He would have told me. I would have been there.*

"Really, Sophie. Do you have to be so vulgar?"

"Yep."

Mom, if it was possible, got even stiffer. "He just made a big announcement. You missed it."

The messages...

Son of a bitch actually did it.

Penelope Gold and her company, The Christmas Experience, were the second prong in the three-prong plan. What was supposed to be a merger had somehow turned into an engagement. Apparently during merger negotiations, Was had fallen in love with Penelope and asked her to marry him. I'd called bullshit on this, but my playboy brother, who usually dated a new woman every week, had been sticking to the story. I hadn't met Penny until this week, and I'd wanted to hate her, but Penny was just too damn nice.

And now they were married.

"Your brother," Mom said, shaking her head with sympathy and concern and every scrap of maternal instinct in her bony body. "He's working so hard. And now married to this... unimpressive girl? I don't like it. I told your father, not that he listened. But I don't like this for your brother. He deserves so much better."

This was the thing with my mom. Every girl was unimpressive. She only saw my brother and father. Like, this was old-generation stuff, right? Only men mattered. Sons and husbands and fathers—my job as a sister and a daughter was to just keep reflecting the best versions of the men in my life out into the world.

Mom had done that her whole life and look where it got her—a husband who'd lied and cheated and whom she was divorcing. And a son who barely tolerated her.

And meanwhile, my hands had calluses from doing my part to turn this company around. I went to all the meetings my brother called for, I followed the cost-saving protocols introduced by the new CFO, and I treated my crew like the family they were to me. And when I overheard a couple of employees bitching about all the changes, I told them to collect their checks and move on. And my favorite show of support—on Thursday nights after work I went up to my brother's office and we kicked our feet up on Dad's old desk and drank a bottle of the good stuff my Dad had hoarded for the end of the world.

But maybe it was because I worked in the back, in the shipping department, and Mom hated that. Because I couldn't even be a girl right. Or maybe it was because I was a girl and so somehow...less in her eyes. I didn't know, and frankly, I was long past caring. I'd tried so hard to get this woman to love me and it didn't matter.

"It wouldn't kill you to support your brother," Mom said, interpreting my silence as not supporting my brother.

"Let's not do this tonight, Mom. We're supposed to be having fun."

"Is that why you're dressed that way?" she asked. Her silver hair reflected the green and red lights and her eyes... well, they reflected what they always reflected when she looked at me.

"Yep," I said.

"It doesn't have anything to do with that boy being back."

Only Mom would call a decorated Marine *that boy*.

"Okay Mom, it's been lots of fun talking to you, but I'm going to go—" I twirled a finger around "—mingle."

"All right, Sophie. Try..."

To act like a Kane. To make her proud. To be less myself. More like my mother. Dignified and quiet and whatever.

"I always do, Mom. Believe it or not, I always do."

I turned and sucked back my champagne, setting my

glass down on an empty table. The champagne was fizzy and sweet, and went to my knees and my head at the same time. A fast drink on an empty stomach was one of my favorite things.

Now I needed to find my brother.

And Sam. Really, I just wanted to find Sam.

The band was good. They were doing swingy-dancey versions of Christmas songs and there were a few people out on the floor. Rhonda who worked the front desk and Romeo from the warehouse clearly had moves.

Sam was nowhere to be found. Maybe he wasn't here? He'd said he was coming and he was the kind of guy who showed up when he said he would. Oh man, he'd have something to say when he found out about Wes and Penny.

I saw Penny standing alone looking like a zillion bucks in a red dress.

My sister-in-law. Well, no time like the present to welcome her into the family. I whisked her away from the bar and behind the huge Christmas tree. Which was as close to privacy as we were going to get.

"So you did it," I said, trying not to sound accusatory. "You married my brother."

"You look really nice," she said to me, and I was totally thrown for a loop. She was all kinds of still waters running deep. She was hard to get a read on. But when she pushed her glasses up higher on her nose, she revealed some of her nerves, and when she did that...she was impossible not to like.

"Do you really mean that?" I asked.

"Yes, I do."

I shook my head. Damn it. I liked her and there was more to this engagement and marriage than anyone was being told. "You really are nice," I said. "My brother doesn't deserve you."

"Are you here with a date?" she asked me, carefully hedging the compliment.

"No. I don't have a date." What I had was a plan. And a thong.

"Those two," Penny said, nudging my arm discreetly and tilting her head to the wall behind her. "No, don't look, he'll see."

"W.B.?" I asked, not bothering at all to be discreet. The third prong in my brother's plan was the new CFO, W.B. Darling. W.B. found out my father was embezzling from the company, which had helped save the company but nearly torn our family apart. W.B. was a good guy for a man who had a spreadsheet shoved up his butt. Joy walked past him without a word and W.B. broke away from the wall to follow. Very interesting.

"Yes. Him and Joy. There's something going on there, don't you think?" Penny asked.

Yes! Yes, I did think, as a matter of fact. But Joy was not saying a word about W.B.

"I think Joy is into him, but she says she isn't," I said.

"She seems mad at him."

"Why would she be mad at him?"

"It's just a hunch," Penny said.

Over her shoulder I saw half my warehouse crew walking over with napkins wrapped around fresh bottles of beer. That's how fancy this party was. The bartenders put napkins around the beer so your hand didn't get wet and cold. And they were going to come grill Penny and give her a hard time that she didn't deserve on the night of her wedding.

"All right," I said. "Welcome to the family and all that.

Don't get cornered by my mom." With that plum bit of advice I took one for the team and went to intercept my crew.

"Holy shit, Sophie, is that you?" Joe Arben asked.

"Yeah, it's me," I said, like it was every day I stood there looking the way I did. "What about it?"

Joe whistled, a long, low wolf whistle and maybe at another time, in another boss/employee situation, I'd have had to bust some heads over that, but at that moment I took it as a compliment. And let me tell you, I tried real hard not to look at Joe, but I was very aware that he was looking at me.

He was a kid, nineteen years old, a fairly new hire, and he had made his interest in me obvious. But Joe was also the kind of guy who was interested in anything with boobs. So it wasn't personal. Even though no one ever looked at me that way. Anyway, I was not letting it go to my head. He was charming and sweet and my employee, and his attention embarrassed me.

So I ignored him.

Sort of.

"Damn girl," he said. "You are the hottest thing here."

I could feel myself blushing. "How many girls has he said that to?" I asked Joe's friend Zavier.

"None," Zavier said, sipping from his beer, his eyebrow cocked.

I rolled my eyes.

"You having a good time?" I asked the guys.

"This is a real good party, Soph." Paul Sorvinski, who'd been working in the warehouse for as long as I could remember, carried two plates of shrimp and satay and mini quiches. His wife, the always smiling Marie, set down two beers so she could hug me tight around my neck.

"You look so nice," she said.

"Thank you."

"When you're ready to dance," Joe said, lifting his beer, putting a little innuendo on *dance*, "you know where I am."

I did a super-awkward smile-laugh-shrug combo that was kind of my trademark and quickly got out of there. More champagne was needed, but where was one of those snappily dressed waiters with trays of it when you needed one?

When we renovated the top floor to make it a fancy-shmancy party room, we'd put in an old bar that the designer unearthed out of a condemned Denver hotel. It was one of those fancy Wild West mahogany bars that had actual bullet holes in it. I found my way to the side of it to get another glass of champagne.

And that's when I saw him.

Across the bar, sitting with a beer and talking to two of Joy's glassblowers and Annie in sales, was Fucking Sam Porter.

3

———

He wasn't in a suit. Not even a tie. Just a dress shirt that was too big, because he'd lost weight on his last deployment. His jet-black hair was still jarhead short, which revealed the long, jagged scar over his ear (that he got as a kid climbing a tree), and another one on the back of his skull that was still pink and raised (that he got in mysterious circumstances on his last top-secret deployment, and was part of why he was home and part of why he'd lost so much weight). A third scar (something he'd gotten in a bar fight defending—as he claimed—Wes's honor) sliced through his eyebrow. As I watched, he ran his hands over his head, front to back and back again, the way he always did when he was agitated.

It was the party. He didn't like crowds.

One of the glassblowers tipped her head back and laughed a real tinkly laugh at something Sam said, which was dubious because Sam was not at all funny, and then she put her hand on Sam's arm.

Looking away, I drained half my glass of champagne. I heard him laugh. Laugh at something the glassblower said.

The rare, low rumble of it cut through the music and the distance and my heart.

I'd been ten when Wes found Sam and brought him home. Or maybe it was Sam who'd found Wes, just when they needed each other. Hardly mattered. They met and became inseparable. Brothers more than friends. And Sam treated me like he was another older brother. Part fierce protector, part ambivalent friend, part annoyed family member. And I was pretty stupid, but I wasn't *so* stupid as to say I fell in love with him when I was ten and he was fifteen. (No, I managed to save that for a few years). The first time I saw him he'd had a black eye and a ripped shirt, and he'd eaten fistfuls of the microwave popcorn I'd popped. And then Mom had come home and while Wes and I argued about where to hide Sam, Sam sneaked out the back door taking a silver candlestick with him.

A move that had been so scandalous to me when I was ten. Now I *loved* it. Loved that he took that candlestick, got some food and his mom some antibiotics for a sinus infection that wasn't going away and a pair of slick new tennis shoes. I loved that he took that candlestick and came back the next day. For Wes. And more popcorn.

"You can stay," Wes had told Sam. "But you can't steal. My mom finds out and she'll have you arrested or something. So you ask me for anything and it's yours, but you can't steal."

They smacked hands and ran off to do very thrilling and mysterious fifteen-year-old boy stuff, and I'd run after them as fast as my legs could carry me.

And then, suddenly, Sam was just there. More often than not. He asked for money one other time, and Wes and I pooled what we had in our birthday stashes and gave it to him. A thousand bucks.

Wes had said it was for bail for his dad.

Sam never said anything, but six months later he paid us back. I have no idea what he did to make that money.

Yeah, I didn't fall in love with him then. Or when he enlisted three years later, and Wes and I saw him off. Sam hugged me so hard my feet were lifted up off the ground, and he whispered, all rough and gruff in my ear, "Stay safe, kid."

Two years later, I didn't make the cheerleading team in high school and Wes must have told him. And out of the blue Sam wrote me a letter telling me that cheerleaders were lame and the fun at football games was always under the bleachers. Not on the field.

He took the time and the care to try and make me feel better about stupid high school shit by writing a letter from some place in Iraq. I mean...maybe I fell a little in love with him because of that letter. We started playing video games on-line after that.

Wes didn't know. I never told him and neither did Sam. Our friendship was a tiny little secret we kept. Or, I did. Maybe Sam was embarrassed and that's why he kept his mouth shut.

But the real moment, the final kill shot, had been the year he came home and could no longer tell us where he was stationed. Or what he did there.

I found him in the middle of the night in the kitchen— our kitchen. The Kane family kitchen. Wes had his own place at that point but he was away on business.

So, he'd come to me.

And his eyes were dark and his mouth was different.

"Is this okay?" he asked. "Me being here."

"Always," I said, surprised by how much I meant it. By how much I *wanted* it.

And I could tell something had happened. Something big. Something awful. Something he couldn't tell me about and somehow he couldn't handle on his own.

I popped popcorn he didn't eat. Made tea he didn't drink. Told stories until he smiled. Jokes until he laughed. I stayed at the kitchen island, and by the time the sun came up I was twenty years old and I was deeply in love with my brother's best friend.

I'd thought it would go away. He got deployed again and I wrote him and he wrote me back. We played video games. He showed up, he vanished again.

I got my own apartment, and when he was home he'd come over and played Skyrim all day with me. We ordered pizzas and drank beer like nothing was different, but the entire time my body thrummed with the nearness of him. Tracking him around my apartment. Around my life.

Years I'd spent loving this guy and he didn't know? Didn't see? Was I so invisible? Or was he pretending? And why did that feel so much worse?

Now he was back with that fresh pink scar.

And I was dressed up in the shoes and the thong because I just couldn't take it anymore.

I might end up in flames, but I was taking a shot.

The last of the champagne went down in one big gulp and I turned, ready to confront the love of my life.

Only to find Sam standing next to me.

"Jesus," I shouted and dropped the glass. Which he caught—because of course he did—and set with a quiet click on the bar. "Sam, you can't sneak up on a person."

"A second ago you were staring at me."

"Well, I was just wondering who the guy was who didn't get the memo about the dress code."

"This was all I had," he said. Which wasn't true. I'd seen

him in his dress blues with the sword and everything. But he was making a point that I should shut up about his clothes.

"I'm surprised you came," I said, shifting my body just slightly away from his because I could feel the heat from him. I could feel the iron strength of his arm beneath the too-big sleeve of his shirt. And it was distracting. And I didn't want to be distracted from telling him how much I wanted to see him without that shirt.

Yeah. It didn't make much sense to me, either, but that was the effect he had on me. He turned me upside down just being in the room.

"I love a party," he said with a tilt of his lip—the illusion of a smile. I gave him my whole smile in return. Which was how the scales balanced between us. He gave me nearly nothing and I gave him everything I had.

"Me too," I lied, the same way he'd just lied to me, and when our eyes met, a certain kind of understanding blazed in the space between us. *I know you. And you know me. And I've never felt this way, ever. And I don't know how to live if you don't feel the same way.*

"We could leave," Sam said. "Go back to your place. Kill some dragons. Steal some scrolls."

"My brother would kill us."

"You missed the announcement."

"He really did it, huh?"

"He really did."

"Were you...there? Like...at the ceremony?"

"No, Soph. He didn't have anyone there." It was in his tone of voice, he knew what I was asking and why.

"Do you think it's real?" I asked.

Sam grunted. And in the Sam Porter translation app that I had built and refined over years of knowing him, I knew that what he meant was, *We'll see and I doubt it and sometimes you're right about people but I'm not going to admit that at this moment and I'm just worried about my best friend who has been acting like a mad man since taking over the company.*

I poked him in his rock-hard side and he jerked back, smiling.

"Jesus, kid. I don't know what to think."

The *kid* stung. Not gonna lie.

"What a liar you are," I said, laughing at him. "He's always told you more than he's told me. Not that I'm bothered."

"You are so bothered."

"I am! Why does he do that?"

"He's asked us to trust him. Let's just...do that."

"I like Penelope," I said. With a sudden pang, thinking about that conversation we'd had, I wished I'd cut her a break earlier. Wished I could take back some of the things I'd said. Thought, even.

"Food's good. Have you had any?" he asked, and I smiled at his predictable change of topic.

"Not yet."

"There's a crab thing you'll love. But they go fast."

"I'm not hungry," I said, and he looked at me sideways. Because I was always hungry. Around him I put food in my mouth so I had something to do with my hands. Something to keep me from saying the words I was so scared of saying to him.

"There's a chocolate fountain."

"Really?"

"Yeah. In the corner. You can dip all kinds of stuff in it. There's pretzels."

Sweet and salty, another one of my favorites. How well he knew me was a bruise he kept poking.

And it had not escaped my notice that we'd been

standing here, chatting and looking at each other and breathing the same air, and he hadn't said a single word about how I looked. I glanced down just to make sure I was still wearing a tight, sparkly blue dress.

Yep.

So, should I say something? *Like my dress? Notice anything different about me?* It felt silly. Needy.

"You enjoy your time with the glassblowers?"

"Is that what they are?"

"Indeed."

Had I ever said *indeed* before? Never. This thong was cutting off all the blood to my brain.

"This is quite a party Wes is throwing," he said. "He trying to convince everyone the company isn't bankrupt? Or is it to impress Penny?"

"Both." I shrugged. He took a sip from his bottle of beer.

"Have you talked to him?" I asked.

"Nah. Saw your mom."

"Christmas spirit herself?"

"She hissed at me."

"Well, that's an improvement."

We grinned at each other. I actually couldn't stop. He made me so happy.

"You want a drink?"

I want to know what you think of my dress. I want to know what you think of my ass. Of me.

"Sure."

"Champagne or the usual?"

"You know my usual?"

He turned and ordered a gin and tonic with two limes for me, which was, in fact, my usual, and when he slipped the glass into my hand I broke. I broke right in half.

"Notice anything different about me?" I asked, my voice

strident and loud. It was like I was screaming the question at him.

"You're taller," he said, ordering another beer for himself.

"Well, it's the shoes."

"Your hair is...bigger."

Something went sour in my stomach.

"Your dress is very...bright."

It was reflecting the light from the dance floor. I was a beautiful blue disco ball. But I didn't have the breath to say that. "You've never seen me in a dress."

"Yeah." He laughed and took a huge gulp of his beer, his eyes going across the bar to where the glassblowers were standing. "It's a little weird."

It was like one of those balloons shot in slow motion. That was actually the feeling in my stomach. In my body. I felt the terrible puncture and the slow explosion, like every part of me had lost connection to every other part of me. I gasped and gasped again, and he looked at me and then looked away.

"So, what are the names of the glassblowers?" he asked.

"I don't...I don't know," I said, trying to gather myself up. Finding an arm over there and a leg over there, the beating of my weak heart right there at his feet.

"The blonde is hot."

Tears. I hadn't cried since we got the phone call from his mother three months ago that Sam had been hurt and that he was unconscious and alone a million miles away.

Humiliated, I blinked the burning tears back, but it wasn't working.

There. That's the answer. He never saw you like that. Never thought of you like that.

"Sophie?" he said, like I'd chocked on an olive pit. "You all right?"

If I opened my mouth I wasn't sure what I would say. If I opened my mouth I wasn't sure I wouldn't sob, and it had already been a bad night. The stuff nightmares were made of. I didn't have to go and add more to it. Crying because of Fucking Sam Porter was one thing. Crying in front of him was the kind of thing I would never recover from.

So I sucked back that gin and tonic like it was medicine for a broken heart.

"Hey, careful—"

Yeah. Fuck him and his worry. I turned on my fancy high heel and got the hell away from him before I could do anything else I might regret. Blindly, I circulated back through the shadows, looking for my brother. Joy. Anyone who might make this feeling go away, but then I realized, it wouldn't. It would never go away.

The humiliation shifted, making room for the grief. The bone-deep grief that the man I loved with my whole self didn't feel at all the same way about me.

There was only one thing to do—leave.

4

———

S am

Though it was getting harder and harder to tell what

T HAT...

That had been the right thing to do. 100%.

I was sure of it.

Though it was getting harder and harder to tell what was right and what was wrong when it came to Sophie Kane. When she'd been a kid, it had been simple: protect her.

But then she grew up and started looking at me out of the corner of her eye. And she got real interested in me and my damage, and that was a mistake no matter which way I looked at it.

So then the mission became: ignore her. But that was impossible. It was like ignoring a 4th of July Sparkler right in front of your face. A tiny little pivot and I just had to ignore how she felt about me. Which she did a shit job of hiding.

But even that was hard, because a few times I selfishly wallowed in her kindness. Her respect. The bright center of her love.

I know. I'm an asshole.

But, I took some comfort in the fact that I'd tried so hard for years. *For years.* Not to look at her *that* way. See her *that* way. She was my best friend's little sister. She was, if I was honest, probably more of a best friend than my actual best friend.

But goddamn...that dress.

No. That had been the right thing to do. Maybe a little... mean? Like cauterizing a wound. She had to move past this infatuation she had with me. And all I'd done was help her along.

By pretending her beauty was embarrassing.

By pretending she didn't take my fucking breath away.

My stomach was sick. I was going to remember that look on her face for the rest of my life.

Fuck.

At one of the tables full of staff, a man, a boy, really, watched her as she left, tried even to stop her, maybe ask her if she was okay. But she shrugged him off and high tailed it to an elevator.

And then after a few minutes, that same guy put down his beer and took the same path she did. He followed her.

The hair on the back of my neck stood up. Yeah, he could be going to the bathroom or some shit, but he wasn't. I knew it in my gut. Now, was he going to try and comfort her? Or take advantage of a woman in distress? To hurt her? I mean, it seemed unlikely, but the thought, once in my head, was impossible to get rid of.

Because my first rule was still the same. Protect Sophie.

I set down my beer and went after them.

· · ·

Sophie

I got back to the warehouse before the tears came, burning their way out of my eyes, and I tried to take off my shoes, but I couldn't bend down in the dress, and I tried to take off the dress but I couldn't reach the zipper, so I punched my fists down onto my old metal desk and howled. Just howled.

I was fucking trapped in this awful idea of mine. And I couldn't get out.

"Sophie?"

Startled, I turned, only to find Joe Arben standing there in his father's suit.

Oh God.

I closed my eyes and turned back around. Things Can Always Get Worse: The Sophie Kane Story.

"Are you okay?" he asked. I heard him coming down the three stairs from the doorway down to the floor of the warehouse. "I saw you leave and you seemed upset."

"I'm fine," I said, not sounding it.

He was on the cement floor, walking toward me and when his hand touched my elbow I flinched and then covered my face with my hand.

"Sweetheart? What happened?" he whispered. It was nice to be called sweetheart, even though I knew he didn't mean it. He couldn't. I wasn't anyone's sweetheart. I was... plain old Sophie Kane and a fool for trying to be anything else.

"Nothing," I said, pleased that my voice didn't sound drenched in tears. "I'm just...not having a great night."

"What can I do?" he asked. His breath touched my arm and I shivered with a keen pleasure pain. Had I honestly thought *Fucking Sam Porter* was going to take one look at me and pull me into his arms? That he'd take one look and drop his drink and put his hands on me the way that I'd dreamed for a stupid number of years?

"Sophie," Joe breathed again, and his fingers were on my neck. "Beautiful women should not cry at parties."

Yeah, well, I thought, *I'm not beautiful.*

I reached again for the zipper, like my desperation would have made it move somehow but no. It was still out of reach.

"Here," he said. "Can I help you?"

"Unzip my dress?" I all but screeched.

"I just want to help."

"Okay, but...not in a sexy way."

In a get-me-out-of-the-damn-dress way.

"Everything about you is sexy," he said and I rolled my eyes. Honestly, I couldn't deal with all this.

"Please, just get me out of this fucking dress." I hung my head, lifting my hair. *It looks like you've rolled in hay.* I flinched at the memory. What had I been thinking? Like a dress could change anything. Makeup.

A stupid thong.

I felt Joe's fingers against my skin and the slow unzipping of my dress was silent, but his breathing was loud.

Was this real? I wondered. I mean, it seemed obvious. But what if I was wrong. The way I was wrong about everything. It suddenly felt like a trick. A joke he might play on me. And I shrank inside my skin. Tears burning again.

The door to the warehouse clanged and I heard the scuff of a shoe on the cement of the steps. I turned, only to find Fucking Sam Porter sitting on the top step, his elbows braced on his knees. Totally casual. Just having a seat. Taking in the sights.

But his face was ominously still.

My dress gaped around my body, the shoulder strap slipping down my arm, and I put my hand to my chest, holding the sequins against my boobs so I wasn't flashing Sam and Joe.

"What the fuck, man?" Joe said, bristling as he stood in front of me as if to protect me from Sam's eyes.

"Don't let me stop you," Sam said, waving his hand at us like none of this—me half naked, Joe's hands on my skin, Sam sitting there *watching*—meant anything. "Seemed like things were just getting good."

My cheeks blazed red hot.

"Get the fuck out!" Joe said, taking a step toward Sam, and I finally found my voice because Joe didn't need to get a beatdown just for trying to protect me. Because Joe was young and strong and tough, but Sam was some kind of super soldier with blood on his hands. The more casual he acted, the more lethal he could be. I'd seen him, in a bar fight years ago, pulverize a guy who wouldn't take no for an answer from a girl in a back booth, and Sam had been whistling as he walked over to the guy.

He wasn't whistling now, but he did stretch out his legs, leaning back against the landing like he was sitting by a goddamn river.

"Joe," I said, holding the dress against my chest. "It's... fine. Everything's fine. Why don't you go back to the party?"

He looked back at me, aghast. "I'm not leaving you here with some creeper."

"He's not a creeper," I said. "He's my brother's best friend."

"That don't mean he's not an asshole."

A harsh laugh scraped my throat.

"I'm an asshole," Sam said. He was using his military

voice. Firm, but kind of soft, too. Like he understood every-thing Joe was feeling, like suddenly he and Joe were in something together. It was the voice I imagined convinced men to follow him into the shitty places where they might get hurt or killed. "But I'm not going to hurt Soph. Go on back to the party."

Joe looked back at me. *He really was a good guy.* And I gave him my very best smile. My Sophie Kane special. *Nothing hurts because I'm as tough as they come.*

But inside, all my stupid dreams and wishes had broken edges, and they were sharp and cutting me to pieces.

"Okay," Joe finally said, shaking his head, like he just didn't understand why I wasn't picking him, and honestly, I was beginning to wonder the same thing. "But if this fucker does one thing you don't want him to—"

Like laugh in my face. Like tell me I look weird. Yeah, he'd already done that. I couldn't imagine there were all that many ways left he could hurt me.

"He won't," I said at the very same time Sam said, "I won't."

Joe walked up the steps, giving Sam a death glare in an effort to provoke him into standing up and throwing a punch, and I wanted to tell Joe to save his energy. Sam Porter couldn't be provoked. There was no stick I'd ever seen that got Sam to do anything he didn't want to do.

The door closed behind Joe and the silence in the ware-house was *deafening.*

"Go back to the party, Sam," I said and turned away. My clothes were on my desk. My hoodie and jeans, and I wanted to take off this dress so bad, but I was frozen by not wanting to reveal even an inch more of myself to him.

"He was touching you."

Sam's voice was practically in my ear and I whirled back

around, still clutching the dress to my chest, only to find him a foot away. Not even. Close enough I could see the green in his eyes. The edge of that scar through his eyebrow. The muscle ticking in his jaw.

"Joe's harmless," I said, exhausted by...everything. "Please go, Sam."

"Did you want him to touch you?"

No, asshole, I wished I was brave enough to say. *I wanted you to touch me but my being beautiful was too fucking weird for you.*

Better late than never, the anger I'd been waiting for welled up in me like a sail catching wind, and my tears and my humiliation and hurt feelings were flattened by my rage.

"That's none of your fucking business, Sam! What were you doing coming down here and watching me?"

He stepped closer, the muscle in his jaw popping like he had rocks in it he was trying to crush. "Did. You. Want. Him. To. Touch. You?"

"Yep," I lied. "I did. I fucking wanted Joe to touch me. What the hell do you care?"

"Is that why you wore the dress? Why you look like that? For him?" He stepped forward, crowding me into the desk at my back. I could feel the heat of his body on the bare skin of my chest, where I was holding the dress against my body.

I shoved at him with my elbow. "Stop crowding me."

"Then answer," he said. "You make yourself look like that for him?"

He said it like I'd rolled in dog shit. Like I'd put on a clown costume and embarrassed myself.

Like I was going to tell him. Like I was going to give him the knives to use against me. But he wasn't budging. Standing there like he had the right. Like he was owed my answers.

So I punched him. The way he taught me when I was sixteen. The crack of it practically echoed and my hand burned and then went numb, and on his face was the bright red imprint of my hand. The violence of it was shocking. My blood pounded in my ears.

"Do it again," he growled. Actually growled. I was pissed at him and hiding a disastrous amount of hurt that would have to be dealt with later, but I felt that growl between my legs, where it mattered. Where it rang me like a bell.

And that pissed me off, too. That I could still want him after tonight. After this fucking stunt.

So I did. I hauled off, closed fist, and punched that asshole right in the face, and it wasn't as good as fucking him but it was something. Oh my God, it was me leaving a mark. Me making him see me.

And then, like the universe just couldn't have that, couldn't let this man actually see me for me—literally or figuratively—the lights went out. And the warehouse was plunged into darkness.

5
——————

I jumped. Startled. And his hand came out of the darkness to touch mine. And I flinched away from him. My body wired with adrenaline.

"The power went out," I said. Inane, but I could feel him close. "The snow."

"It will come back on."

He was closer. His hand squeezed my fist.

"You want to hit me again?" he asked.

"Maybe."

And then, suddenly he wasn't a foot away, he was on me. I couldn't see him. But I felt him. Everywhere. His skin touching mine, and it was so much, too much, and not at all enough all at once.

He slipped his hand around my body. I gasped at the scrape of his calluses against the tender skin of my lower back. In the dark, not being able to see him, I could feel all of him.

He's touching me. Fucking Sam Porter is touching me.

He picked me up, up off my high heels, and stepped forward so I was sitting on my desk. The jar of pens and my sticky notes, the calendar, he pushed everything to the floor. It all clattered in the dark.

"What are you doing?" I gasped.

"Giving you what you want."

"You don't know what I want, you—"

He kissed me. I mean, it took a second for it all to register, but he was *kissing* me. Consuming me. I'd been imagining our first kiss for years. I'd practiced it into the pillow on my teenage bed so many times that sometimes it felt like it had already happened. The careful clumsiness of it. The tenderness. I was sure our first kiss would be so sweet. The sweetest.

Yeah. This kiss wasn't that. At all. This kiss was savage. His tongue in my mouth. His hand at my jaw, holding me still, holding me open. His other hand on my back, holding me like a steel girder so I couldn't move away.

"Fuck," he said into my mouth, and I didn't know what was going on. I couldn't process anything except Fucking Sam Porter was kissing me like he wanted to destroy me and save me all at once.

And the darkness made it somehow possible.

But there was something about this kiss, deep in its core, that didn't feel right. Like he wouldn't do this if the lights were on. Like if the lights were on, he'd embarrass me like he had earlier. Yeah. That. A guy who says that shit, he doesn't get to kiss me five minutes later. I had some pride. I did. Somewhere.

Stop, I thought. *You have to stop this.*

But It felt good. So good. My devil underwear was absolutely soaked. But my heart and my body would betray me for Sam at the drop of a hat. Much less whatever this kiss was.

A joke? Punishment?

I tore my mouth away, my lips burning. "What..." I breathed, and he was kissing me again and I tried to resist. I did! I gave it a good college try, but I'd been dreaming of this moment for years and my spine–usually so reliable–just melted.

I moaned.

"Yeah," he said into my mouth like I'd done something he liked. Like my surrender was what he wanted.

"Sam," I moaned, I had to stop him. I was going to. For sure. Any second.

"Fuck. Say it again."

"What?"

"My name. Say my fucking name again."

I did not know what was going on and I pushed against his chest, and that hand at my back reached up into my hair, grabbing a handful of the curls.

"Say my fucking name again," he whispered, no longer kissing me. My eyes had adjusted to the darkness and with the faint light coming through the high windows I could see the flash of his teeth, the whites of his eyes. That was all, really. But I imagined his beautiful, deep-set hazel eyes boring into me and I was so powerless. So stupid.

"Sam."

And then he was kissing me again and my hands, which were holding up the dress, wanted to curl around his shoulders. Wanted to pull him closer.

The whole of me wanted to give in.

This could be a trick. A joke. You have to—

"Stop," I finally said, with a bit more power and strength than before. And look, Sam Porter was an asshole, but the guy wasn't that kind of asshole, and he stopped. That hand was still in my hair. His body still crowded mine on the desk. But he wasn't kissing me.

"What are you doing?" I asked. My lips felt ravaged and raw. My heart even worse.

He stepped back and I knew in a heartbeat what he was doing. How this would play out. He'd walk away without giving me any answers. Close himself off to me, and the next time I saw him he'd pretend nothing happened. I couldn't honestly bear it. Not now. Not after *this.*

I grabbed his shirt with both hands, my dress slipping. It wasn't like it fell and I was all bare-boobed, but it slipped enough. I looked down and realized because the way the light came in those windows that he could see me better than I could see him. And my skin was so white, and my dress caught and reflected whatever light it could find.

My eyes adjusted further and I could see his jaw. The hard knot of it.

"Is this a joke?" I asked, because I honestly wasn't sure. "Like, you say what you said upstairs, and then you kiss me like this, and then I'm supposed to laugh. Because you're laughing. At me."

His eyes flew to mine as though he was stunned that I would think that. I'd been so good at hiding my feelings for him for so long, but I just...couldn't anymore. I looked at him with all the love I felt for him. Every bit of it. But with that love came so much pain. And I let him see that, too.

"No," he whispered. "It's not a joke."

"Then what—"

"It's what you want," he said. Him kissing me. Touching me.

"Yeah. But..." A laugh burbled out of me. "Is it what *you* want?" I mean, the guy never did anything he didn't want to do, but this was coming out of left field. "You said I looked weird."

Sam. Fucking Sam Porter stepped forward, pushing my knees out wide, and when the skirt of the dress wouldn't let them go any further he slipped his hands up my thighs.

I gasped. I couldn't help it. His rough palms on my pale,

untouched skin. It was amazing I was still conscious. He pushed the dress up higher, practically to my waist.

"Fuck, Soph," he whispered. And then he pulled me forward against his body. Until it was me, barely covered by damp satin, and him. Hard as a rock beneath his pants.

"I want you," he said, like we were fighting. Like I was disagreeing with him about something.

My eyes might have rolled back in my head.

"You look...beautiful, Soph. So fucking beautiful."

I had about ten million other questions but they were shoved back down my throat by his kiss. You know in those old romance novels when the hero gives the heroine a *punishing* kiss? Yeah. That was this kiss.

His hands on my body were rough. His mouth was rough, the way he pulled me up against him. All of it rough.

He was punishing me for making him feel some kind of way and I was here for it. All day long I was here for it. There was going to be some seriously messy fallout from this. But I was having it. Having him.

Cleanup could come later.

This was my Christmas wish come true.

I wrapped my arms around his shoulders and the rest of my dress slipped down my body. My breasts were there, cold in the warehouse air, and he groaned, cupping them in his palms. And I wanted a thousand words from him to erase his silence over all these years, but wanting Sam to talk was like wanting fish to walk. It just wouldn't happen. So I soaked up all his touch. Convincing myself that whatever happened next and no matter what had happened before— right now he wanted me as much as I wanted him.

He kissed his way from my mouth to my neck, down over my chest to my tits, pulling my nipples into his mouth. "Yes," I groaned. "Oh my God, yes."

"You like that?" he asked, his deep voice like another set of hands on my flesh. I whimpered as he squeezed my breasts together, licking the nipples. Sucking one and then the other. I squirmed and arched against him, the hard press of his cock so good. I reached down and yanked aside my thong, spreading myself just a little, so the next thrust of his cock against me hit my clit.

The pleasure was like electricity through my whole body. I literally shook.

He stopped licking me and I opened my eyes, only to find him watching me. Serious and hot, his mouth swollen, and I realized I'd been kissing him as hard as he was kissing me.

"You can take care of yourself, can't you?"

"You mean...can I make myself come? Sure. Can't you?" I cocked my head at him.

"Make you come?" His lip lifted, the half smile that changed the beat of my heart. "I think I can figure it out."

Oh, this was our old game. I understood him like this. Trash talking over video games and Broncos vs. Bears. Arguing over the last chicken wing, which television series had the worst ending, or who was the best Batman. This was comfortable.

I'd just never been mostly naked while doing it.

"Go for it," I said and then leaned back, bracing one hand behind my body as if this...*presenting* myself to him... was something I'd done before. I even gave him my best Sophie Kane smile, the one that hid all the stains and pains.

But at the sight of my smile, his vanished. And his eyes were dark storms on my body. "We're doing this, Soph," he said. "And there's no going back."

"Well, it looks like you're—"

His hand covered the whole of my pussy. The heel of it

pressing down on my clit, his fingers slipping, just barely, just enough, inside of me, and I couldn't breathe. All the air was gone and his eyes held me so still.

He pushed down harder with his hand, as though he knew that was what I liked. What I needed. That abstract pressure. I whimpered.

"I fucking love that sound, Sophie."

Don't make it again, I thought. But then, of course, the devil, he pressed down on me again. Slipping that big, wide finger of his inside me. So hard and so deep I had to tilt my head back.

"I want that sound, Soph."

"Too bad."

His laughter was dark, devious medicine. My soul, starving for whatever scraps he would give me, soaked it up. My eyes drifted closed as pleasure sparked and sparkled inside of me, growing bright.

No, I thought. *Open your eyes. You don't want to miss this.*

And oh, sweet Jesus, I didn't. Because Fucking Sam Porter was getting down on his knees in front of me, his hands pressing my thighs out wide. He glanced up at me, something unreadable on his face. He licked his lips like he could already taste me, and I felt those delicious forerunners of an orgasm pushing at me. Pulling at me.

His fingers spread me wide and he licked me. Sucked me. Tongued me.

"Oh my God," I groaned. My thighs twitched under his hands and he pushed them out further. His chest settled against me, his palms grabbed my ass, holding me still. Holding me down. Holding me close.

"Make that sound again," he said.

I couldn't even remember which sound he was talking about.

"Make me."

His laugh was dark desire made audible, and my toes curled in my shoes.

"I'm going to make you scream my name."

"Oh my God, now you're talkative guy?"

He laughed again, and even I had to smile, and I'd never been so turned on and so happy all at once. Because it was Sam. Sam made this perfect.

He bent down to put his mouth on me again. Finding all my spots. Every one of my places.

I wrapped my fist in his shirt, but it wasn't enough. I needed his skin. His heat. I needed to put my fingernails against his flesh and hold on tight. I grabbed his neck, lifting my hips, fucking into him and he fucked into me.

"Yes," I moaned and then again. "Please. Please." And again. I might have been screaming it but my entire body squeezed tight, my orgasm in all my muscles, between my legs. In my brain.

My heart.

"Sam." I cried it. Sobbed it.

And had just enough sense to swallow back *I love you*. But only barely.

I opened my eyes, tried to catch my breath. Tried to calm down my heart. Tried not to lose my damn mind.

Sam Porter just went down on me.

He made a groaning noise and kissed the top of my knee, and I realized I had my hand around his head in a death grip. His scar was raised and ridged against my fingers.

"I'm sorry," I said and pulled my hand away. "Did I hurt you?"

"No," he said quietly. Kissed me again. He stood up, his face damp from me, and tomorrow I would be embarrassed about that but right now I loved it. I reached for him. His shoulders were like stones beneath his shirt and I wanted that shirt gone. Off. And I started to pull at it, yanking it from his pants. It took me a second to realize he wasn't helping me. He wasn't ripping it off his body so he could get skin to skin with me.

"Hey," I said, and when he looked up, even in the dark with only that silvery light from the window, I could see that he was gone. In his head. His body was here, but his mind was leaving me.

Retreating to that place of his where I couldn't follow no matter how much I teased or trash talked or insulted him. "No," I said and shook my head.

"We should go," he said. "Back to the party."

"We should get naked, is what we should do."

He shook his head, stepping back, but I had a hold on his shirt and I wasn't letting go. I even put a leg behind his, like I had the strength to keep him close.

"Soph—"

I just went for it, putting my hand against his cock where it strained so hard against his pants. "You said you were going to give me what I want," I said. "I want this." I pressed, squeezed, ran the heel of my hand from his balls to his belt.

I heard the shudder of his breath. The way it broke. Over what sounded like a curse. I could feel him yielding to me, and I understood why he liked it when I did it for him. It was the sweetest surrender.

"Soph," he groaned.

"I like that sound. I want that sound." I squeezed him. In the moonlight my dress was hanging to my waist, the skirt pressed up over my ass. I was all but naked in front of him and I honestly couldn't believe it. He took a shuffling step toward me. His cock twitching.

Yes, I thought. *Yes. This is it. The beginning of us.*

And then the lights flickered and blazed. And there we were, caught like deer in the headlights.

6

———

We looked at each other and then away. He got caught up in the sight of my naked breasts and I got caught up in the sight of my hand on his pants, holding him so privately. A way I'd never held him or touched him before this moment.

I wanted suddenly to laugh. Or say something. But what to say? Always my problem. I didn't know the words to put to any of my feelings.

And just like that, the excitement, the dirty thrill, the stupid, stupid hope in my heart, started to melt away.

And what had been okay in the dark was suddenly strange. I was too naked. He was too dressed. Was that my hand on his cock?

He grabbed my wrist, squeezing for just a second like he might yank me toward him. And I thought, *Yes, please. Do that. Pull me from this moment into the next moment.* But he just lifted my touch away from his body and let go.

"I don't want this," he said, and I blinked. The words not making sense. Not want? He was just on his knees. He was just kissing me, grabbing my ass. What *didn't* he want?

The words...oh God. They settled like punches to my stomach.

"Fuck you Fucking Sam Porter," I snapped, pushing myself off my desk. I stumbled a little in the high heels, my legs unsteady because Sam had made me come so hard my knees were broken. He reached out to steady me, his fingertips against the skin of my waist, and I glared at him so hard he pulled his hand back.

Practically naked, I shoved the dress down off my body. Standing there in a thong and high heels. His eyes swept over me and blazed hot. That was something, at least. A reaction. I pulled my hoodie on over my bare tits and bent over to take off my shoes.

"Get out of here," I said.

He stepped back and didn't leave.

"You have a hearing problem now?" I asked. Almost yelling. I felt some hysterical scream building in me. I'd been embarrassed before. Hair like mine, grades like mine, temper like mine, job like mine. Parents like mine. But this was something else. A whole new level.

"You're going back upstairs?" he asked.

"Yeah," I lied, kicking off my shoes and pulling on my jeans.

"Okay. I'll...see you up there."

"Fantastic." I took my straw hair and pulled it up in a ponytail, still not looking at him. Still willing him into a hole in the earth. But he didn't move. "I need a second, asshole." I glared at him and he nodded.

"I'll be upstairs," he said.

In the silence he left behind I gathered up my crap and grabbed my keys, and in the lobby I headed outside instead of into an elevator. The party would do just fine without me.

All those years of wishing and I'd finally kissed Sam

Porter. And I'd built it up as the happiest thing that could happen to me. The beginning of something. And somehow it felt like the end. I didn't know how we could be friends after this.

My brother was married. And I didn't know what was going on. I felt, oddly, like crying.

The employee parking lot was empty except for my Jeep and a couple of the delivery vans.

And Sam.

Of course. Standing under one of the lights in the parking lot.

"What are you doing?"

"I knew you weren't going to go back up to that party."

"Yeah, well, bully for you."

Sam caught me at the edge of the light. Reaching for me, but stopping himself before actually touching me. But it hardly mattered. I was peeled, raw, inside out. Standing close to him hurt.

"You okay?" he asked, his voice that calm, deep murmur that made it hard to breathe. "Your brother and everything... with us. I just want to be sure you're okay."

I walked right on by him, giving him the finger as I went.

He didn't get to know how I was. Not anymore.

7

Christmas morning used to be one of my favorite days. Not just the presents, which, you know, who doesn't like presents? My dad was very good at trying to buy his family's love and before we caught on, my brother and I were pretty easily bought.

But Christmas was one of the few days my whole family would be in the room together. My dad, whom I'd so rarely seen when I was a kid, would come down unshaven and in his robe. My mom managed to unscrew her lips enough to smile. And Wes. My parents weren't great with tradition, but Wes and I picked up the slack. He used to do this thing where he'd get me a theme gift—the year I was crazy for Pink! He made this scavenger hunt to find the T-shirt, the poster, and the concert tickets he'd bought for me. And every year I bought the craziest, sometimes grossest candy I could find, going so far as to have friends ship things from overseas, and stuffed a stocking full of things to satisfy his legendary sweet tooth.

After Mom and Dad fought and left—Dad for the office, Mom for a bottle of white wine—Wes and I would sit there in the ocean of torn wrapping paper, surrounded by all the trappings of Christmas, and I would think my brother and I were being a family *despite* my parents. And it was enough.

More than enough.

When I got my own place I stopped putting up decorations because it seemed so fake. All those years with our house done up like a snow globe and not a speck of real Christmas spirit to be found. A tree and a wreath didn't make Christmas. People made Christmas. Love made Christmas.

But this Christmas, just when I could have used the comfort of my brother, he and Penny were off somewhere honeymooning. My father was in jail and there was just no way— no way—I was going to my mother's to feel like crap and get the third degree about Wes's marriage. When I didn't have a single answer for her.

Nope.

Not when I was still so raw from what had happened with Sam.

So I found myself performing my one other Christmas tradition. Going to see Sam's mom, Betty. Every year that Sam was overseas I'd gone out to her trailer and taken her an angel. We had a whole thing going with them. Angels to watch over Sam wherever he was. She would make some kind of elaborate baked good and we'd have a cup of coffee and talk about what we'd heard from Sam. Some days I stayed so long we ordered Chinese food and she'd pour me a glass of beer and we'd talk until the sky was full of stars.

It was a nice tradition.

And the truth was, I knew there was a ninety-five percent chance of Sam being at his mom's place, but I was not going to let him scare me off. Or take away the one tradition I had left to me this morning.

I could ignore him.

I don't want this.

I could pretend to ignore him.

Betty lived out at Rustic Ranch, north of the city, and the storm that had blown through last night made getting out there interesting in my Jeep, even with the four-wheel drive. But I was painfully aware that I had nothing else to do. My brother was married. Starting a new family. Work was closed.

Truth be told, I'd never felt so alone.

I got out to Betty's trailer about an hour later than I'd planned, but I knew it didn't matter to her. That woman's open-door policy toward me had kept me sane more times than I could count in the years Sam was serving overseas.

I'd barely knocked before the door was pulled open to reveal Betty in her Mickey Mouse Christmas sweatshirt and the necklace that lit up like little Christmas lights. Betty was a force of nature, and her hair was a silver helmet, unmovable by anything but God.

"There you are, girl!" she said and pulled me into her skinny arms. The trailer was meticulously clean. A tree was covered in blinking lights and dozens of macaroni and glitter ornaments that Sam had made in grade school. Christmas music was playing through the fancy wireless speaker Sam had gotten her for Christmas a few years ago.

Sam had sent me a What's App message from wherever he was fighting whoever he was fighting, asking me if I could help her set it up. She'd been a reluctant convert, but once she realized she could get every Hank Williams Jr. song just by saying his name, she'd quickly gotten the hang of it.

"Sam said there was no way you'd make it out here today on account of all this snow, but I told him he didn't know you as well as I did."

"What's a little snow in the way of my favorite Christmas tradition?" I looked over her shoulder for any glimpse of Sam. No sign, and my shoulders relaxed. Maybe he was wherever my brother was, getting answers my brother couldn't give me. Or shoveling sidewalks for Betty's neighbors or burying himself in ice, never to be seen again. Whatever. He didn't seem to be here.

And that was the best Christmas gift of all.

"That's what I said. I found a new gingerbread cake on the internet this year and I'm not so sure about it, but I figure we'll give it a try."

"I'm sure it's great," I said. And handed her the present. It was one of Joy's designs and I'd asked her to make a little tweak to it specially for Betty. Joy reminded me that she was paid a hundred bucks an hour and I reminded her that we were friends.

"Merry Christmas," I said.

Betty opened the big red bow and dug through the glittery tissue paper that was a part of the new Kane Co. packaging I was trying so hard to get implemented. Betty gasped as she pulled out the ornament. An angel, of course. Made of beautiful clear blown glass with wings as big as my palm and a glass scroll between the wings with gorgeous gilt lettering: *Look after my Sam.*

"Oh my," she gasped, holding the angel up to the light.

"Probably could have used it before his last deployment, huh?" I said, remembering the pain of that phone call from Betty. Those weeks we hadn't known what was going on, or the month we had and it was all so scary. I still felt it, sitting in this warm, cozy house with the knowledge that Sam was home and okay. My heart beating harder. Adrenaline in the back of my throat.

"No, my boy needs watching over all the time. This… honey, this is so beautiful."

"We hired a new artist," I told her as she reverently turned the angel around in her hands, taking in every inch of its artistry. "Joy. She made it."

"Just for me?"

I smiled at her and was so glad I'd come out here. So glad I had a chance to make her happy like this. To make anyone happy like this. I didn't need presents. I just needed to give presents.

"My girl," she whispered, tears in her eyes, and I hugged her, taking in the ginger smell of her. "Come, sit, sit!" she said. "I've got a pot on and we can try this gingerbread thing I made."

"Gingerbread thing sounds great."

I sat down at the Formica table in a patch of watery sunshine beaming through the snow melting down the window.

"So," Betty yelled from the kitchen. "Your brother up and did it, huh?"

"He got hitched."

"You figure he's just trying to save the company or is he really in love with that girl?"

"I don't know. He's pretty tight-lipped about the whole thing."

"Oh, you don't have to tell me," Betty said, coming in with a plate of cake that she set on the table. She went back into the kitchen and I knew from experience there was no point in asking if I could help. She came back out with two cups of coffee. Mine, I knew, would be made just the way I liked. A little milk. Heaps of sugar. "I got one of those tight-lipped men living in this trailer. Swear Sam came back from that party last night slamming doors like they'd offended him."

I barely flinched when she said his name, and I forced myself not to think what had happened with me was what had made him so upset. The news of the marriage, of course. He was upset about that. We were all upset about that.

"Does he love her?" Betty asked. "Your brother?"

"I don't know," I said. "I think he likes her a lot. I just hope she doesn't hurt him." My biggest fear for him was that he'd end up in a marriage like my parents'. As far as I could tell, Penny was nothing like my mother, but living your life without love...man, that could turn anyone hostile.

For a second, the ache of Sam's hands on my body squeezed my stomach. How stupid I'd been to believe for even a moment that I could have love and sex like that with my brother's best friend. Who got that, really?

"You all right, honey?" Betty asked, putting her hand over mine.

"Good. Just, you know, thinking about Wes."

"Well, let's only think good thoughts," Betty said, doing what she always did and pushing us into positive territory. Suddenly I remembered coming over here with Wes when I was younger. It had been Sam's first deployment and I'd been frantic with worry—couldn't stop crying. Carrying on like the guy was already hurt somewhere instead of just getting yelled at in basic training. Betty had sat me down on her big, saggy floral couch and told Wes to make me some hot chocolate, and she let me cry and say out loud all the things I was scared of.

"Now that you've said all that," she'd whispered. "Let's say all the good things we want to happen to him."

And we'd filled our heads and our hearts with good

things. Until we were laughing and my tears were dry and Wes came out with hot cocoa he'd barely stirred so it was all chewy.

"I'd like him to love Penny. And for her to love him," I said. "Real love, you know?"

She nodded, and I realized that between my parents and Betty's own terrible relationship with Sam's father, we didn't actually have much proof of "real love."

"I just want my brother to be happy," I said.

"Happy sounds good," she said. "We could use a little bit of that around this home, too."

I tried real hard not to perk right up. But the fact that Betty was talking about Sam meant he was not here. I rested easy in my chair and took a sip of my perfect coffee. "Sam's not happy?"

"He's just at loose ends, I think. I don't know that he spent much time thinking about what he would do after serving. And now here we are." She looked up at me and there was something so still in her that I set down my coffee.

"He's not going back?"

She shook her head.

"Is it because of the injury?"

"It's his story to tell and I won't say anything more, but I'm worried, and since you two are such good friends I think you should know, too."

"You're freaking me out, Betty."

"He has nightmares," she whispered. "Insomnia. And he's short-tempered and he won't let me hug him. Or help him."

"PTSD?"

"Yeah, sure," she said. "For about five years. But this is something else..."

Grief and worry settled in my stomach. There was a cost

to what the country asked Sam to do. What he'd signed up to do. And I hated that that cost was so high. And I hated that what had happened during the party made our friendship so strange and maybe...maybe impossible too?

Fuck. I thought. *Just...fuck.*

"Come on, enough sad things. He's home. Your brother is married."

"You have cake!"

"I have cake!" Betty said, lifting her hands in the air, and suddenly we were both laughing. Because we had amazing things to be grateful for, not the least of which was each other.

"Thank you," I said, feeling emotional.

"Thank *you,* honey," she said, grabbing my hand. "All these years coming out here when you didn't have to. Bringing me the angels, giving me things to look forward to. You've been a blessing."

I had to remind myself that just because I'd grown up without much love didn't mean I couldn't recognize it when it came my way. And this was love.

"Are you going to let me have some cake?" I asked.

"Well, you're excited about it now, but the recipe called it *out of the ordinary* and they weren't lying. There's so much ginger it burns a little."

"Burns?" I asked and took a piece of the moist, dark cake with the thin white glaze over top. "That's exactly how I like my cake," I joked. I took a bite and she wasn't kidding. There was a lot going on in that cake.

"Oh my gosh," I said. "That's..."

"Painful?" she asked, trying her own.

"Interesting?"

"One of the reviews called it difficult."

I went back for another bite. "It grows on you," I said.

"That's because you like difficult things."

She laughed, and so I did too, and of course that's when Sam walked in the front door, letting in a blast of cold air that just ruined everything.

He had been out shoveling snow. He wore his big Carhartt coveralls and a black hat that made his face look even redder. He saw me sitting there and looked away. Kicked his boots off on the plastic mat.

"Don't you go bringing in all that wet!" Betty said.

"I'm trying not to," Sam said, and I took a big sip of coffee. What was the deal with his voice and my heart? It was like one of those paddles they used on heart attack victims. It made me all haywire.

"Look who came to visit!" Betty cried, gesturing towards me like she was Vanna White and I was the letter E.

"Hi, Sophie," he said, looking up at me through his black lashes and then away like he couldn't stand the sight of me.

"Sam."

"Merry Christmas," he said.

"You too." I was trying so hard to sound normal and cheerful but somehow I just sounded like one of the Chipmunks. Betty looked between us, like she was well aware of the strange undercurrent we couldn't hide. Or maybe it was just me.

"You're in time for some cake," Betty said.

He took off his boots and came into the trailer in his socks. He filled up the whole space. "I'm gonna hop in the shower."

Yeah, that was the final straw. I wasn't going to sit here while a few thin walls away Sam was getting naked and running soapy hands up and down the body he did not want me to touch.

I jumped to my feet. "I should get going," I said. Both of

them stared at me, knowing I was lying. "My mom's expecting me."

"Oh. Well. You want to take her some cake?" Betty asked. She seemed crestfallen that I was cutting short our visit, and I realized this was just one more thing that was ruined by what Sam and I had done last night. What I had done.

I'd ruined everything I loved. Everything that mattered in my life. Except Wes. Suddenly, I felt outrageously alone. And it was all my own doing.

"No thanks. You keep the cake. Sam'll eat it. Sam will eat anything," I said and kissed Betty's cheek. I grabbed my coat and took the long way around Sam who stood in the middle of the room, dominating the space, taking up all the air with his black knit cap and his frown.

"Merry Christmas, Sam," I managed to whisper.

"You too, Soph."

I got out of that trailer like the Grinch was chasing me.

8

———

S^{am}

The thing about my job, my *old* job, was that it was mostly about waiting. The recruiters don't tell you that. The drill sergeants, when they're screaming at you, don't mention it. But by the time your LT is leading you into the darkest of dark, you're beginning to understand.

The job is about waiting.

That it's learning how to count backward from a hundred in Farsi and playing twenty million rounds of Never Have I Ever with your spotter. It's about getting so still and quiet in your brain that the minutes stop feeling like they're burying you. It's about waiting so long that action actually feels strange. Waiting so long that training takes over and you're halfway into action before you even realize what you're doing.

Stillness and waiting—that was half the job.

And I was so good at it that it was really hard to stop. To remember how to move. To act.

Sophie left the trailer, the sound of her Jeep starting up clear through the snow and the walls of Mom's trailer.

And I stood there, listening, my head cocked, wondering if there was a problem with her timing belt and thinking I should look at it sometime because she was so bad at taking her Jeep in for service.

"Well, what the hell did you do?" Mom asked, her hands on her hips, her eyes spitting mad.

Something I've been trying not to do for five years.

That was the hard-core truth, right there. But I wasn't telling my mom that. I wasn't telling anyone that.

"We got in a fight last night," I said.

Mom made a sound in her throat that meant *bullshit*.

I took off the black hat and scratched the scar tissue at the back of my head.

"That girl is all alone this year on Christmas—"

"Mom."

"I was going to invite her to dinner."

"I know," I sighed.

The other part of my job? Regret.

I knew more than I wanted to about regret. I knew its face and its size. I knew how it felt like the kickback of a M110 against my shoulder .06 seconds after I pulled the trigger. "You want me to go get her back?"

"I want you to make it right, whatever it was that went wrong."

I looked up at my mom's face and I remembered every bit of regret I'd felt as a kid when I couldn't keep her safe. Not from my dad. Not from poverty. Not from me.

"Oh, honey," she said, coming forward to touch me. She moved slowly so I could lurch back if I needed to, but I held myself still and let it happen. She touched my cheek and my hand, and her smile was the safest place I knew. "You're a big dummy."

I was shocked for a second and then I laughed. "You're not wrong," I said. "But to what exactly are you referring?"

"You and Sophie Kane."

I stiffened. There was no me and Sophie Kane. Never could be. I'd had ten minutes with her in the dark last night and even that was stolen. Stolen time. Stolen touch. My hand clenched against the remembered feel of her, like I could hold the memory tight in my fist. She was not mine to have.

"I've been watching you watch her for years now, Sam," Mom said. I shook my head and she lifted her hands. "That's all I'm saying. That girl's alone and I was going to feed her dinner."

I took a deep breath and held it, letting it out slow. Trying to get my heartbeat to stop pounding. Meditation was supposed to help with some of the PTSD, and I was trying my hardest.

"Wrap some up," I said to my mom, who was no doubt expecting me to make this offer. "I'll take it to her."

Ten minutes later I was in my old truck, taking half a chicken potpie and a green salad with the dressing in a little mason jar over to Sophie's place. Determined—*determined*—not to touch her again.

And to try and make things right.

Sophie

. . .

WELL, crap. I had nothing to do. My place was clean; I kept it that way. My brother's phone went right to voice mail. My gym was closed so I couldn't even work out to eat up some time and burn off this energy. So I sat down in my beanbag chair, fired up my PlayStation, and got lost in my video game.

So lost I didn't hear the knock on the door until it was an absolute pound that shook the walls.

"Jesus," I muttered, tossing the controller down. "I have neighbors."

There was only a handful of people who would be knocking on my door on Christmas Day and one of them was on a honeymoon, the other finger-banged me and then told me he didn't want me, and the other one was my mother. So I schooled my face into something polite, expecting the worst, and yanked open the door only to find Sam standing there.

Snow fell down on his black hat and the shoulders of his Carhartt coveralls, and he carried a cardboard box.

Say something smart. Clever. Say something cool.
"Hi."

Nice one.

"Hi. You want this?" he asked and then shoved the box toward me. "It's dinner. Mom wanted you to stay."

"Oh." I took the box. "She didn't have to do that."

"You know Mom."

"You want to come in?" I asked, baffled and slightly tortured by his being here. His eyes took in my body, one long sweeping gaze like he was checking for enemies, and I'd never been so aware of my tiny sleep shorts and my just-over-the-knee cozy socks. A Kane Co. sweatshirt rounded out the whole look.

"I'm going to shovel," he said, jerking a thumb back at

the parking area where all my neighbors' cars were buried under snow and ice.

"It's still snowing," I said.

"Better to get ahead of it," he said, and that, it seemed, was that. He turned around, took the stairs down to where his truck was parked and pulled out his shovel.

Oh my God, I thought. *How Fucking Sam Porter could Sam Porter be?*

The wind was freezing against my bare thighs, so I shut the door and set the box down on the island in my kitchen. There was a tinfoil-wrapped pie tin that smelled like Betty's famous chicken potpie, and I was plenty grateful for that, as well as for the salad in a plastic container and the separate jar of dressing.

But also in the box was a bright blue wrapped package with a silver ribbon.

A Christmas present.

A long time ago I'd established with Betty that the cake, the coffee, and the safe and lovely place to go on Christmas was gift enough from her, so that present could only be from Sam.

I touched the silver ribbon, stretching a curly strand of it straight and then letting go. In my bedroom I had a present for Sam, too. A new headset for when we gamed together. His piece of crap had been left overseas when he'd gotten hurt and I'd gotten him the model he'd had his eye on forever.

Of course, I'd gotten it for him before the whole warehouse incident.

I'd been trying to—if not forget, at least stop remembering—what had happened between us. What he'd done to me. How his hands had felt on my skin, his mouth on my body...

Fuck.

Nope. No. I was not going to sit around getting turned on by memories of him. I wasn't going to sit in my own house and be agitated by this gift. As a rule I wasn't a big drinker. Hangovers were the worst. But if there was a day for a few cocktails it was my All Alone on Christmas Day day. I had a bottle of good gin, some tonic, and a few hard limes. I fixed myself a strong one and sat back down to my game.

Ignoring the gift.

But then I couldn't ignore the gift.

I paused my game and contemplated the pretty wrapped box on my island. Two choices. I could just throw it away. That seemed like a waste of a good gift. Or I could open it. But that seemed dangerous. Foolish, maybe, for a girl trying real hard to eradicate the roots of her years-long infatuation with her brother's best friend.

What I really couldn't do was ignore it. *That* I was failing miserably at. So I picked up the box and put it outside my door. In the cold. Out of sight. Not throwing it away, per se. But not having it in the apartment either.

After that, the first cocktail went down pretty smooth so I made another and then put the potpie in the oven to heat up. This day wasn't so bad.

Sam

THE GIFT WAS outside her door. Snow burying the blue wrapping paper, dampening the ribbons. Perhaps I should have expected that.

Fuck. I really did ruin everything.

I threw the shovel back in the truck and took the steps

up to her apartment. I dusted off the snow on the present as best I could and knocked on her door. Sophie should have presents on Christmas Day and I knew she would like these. I'd known it the second I saw them in the market in Ankara. The woman who made them even showed me how to use them and I'd imagined showing Sophie. How close I would have to stand to her. How she would feel under my hands.

That's probably why I bought them.

And she might not want them, she certainly didn't want me to touch her, but Sophie Kane should have a Christmas present on Christmas.

I knocked. Waited. Hoped she wasn't changing out of those short shorts. Really hoped she wasn't changing out of those just-over-the-knee bright red socks. Knocked again.

The door opened and she stood there (socks and shorts intact), hair a wild, curly mess over her shoulders and around her head. I wondered, for maybe the millionth time, how some guy hadn't snapped this girl up. Put her in his bed and hadn't let her out except to get food when they'd fucked themselves close to starvation.

That Joe guy wanted to. I could smell it on him.

"Sam," she said, trying to sound firm but only sounding angry. "You done shoveling?"

I nodded and held out the present. "This is for you."

"I..." She licked her lips and inside my coveralls I went hard in a heartbeat. "I don't think I want it."

I deserved that. I deserved everything she wanted to throw at me. "It's Christmas Day."

"I know."

"Do you have other presents?" Her apartment, as usual, was completely empty of Christmas. Like it was a holiday that happened around her. Not for her.

She took in a deep breath through her nose. "Not...here."

I held out the box. "You deserve presents on Christmas Day, Soph." She was still hesitant. "How about if I let you yell at me while you open it?" I smiled at her, willing that she take the offer. I saw over her shoulder the bottle of gin and the 2 liter of Tonic. "I'll make you a drink."

"I can make my own drinks."

"I'll let you make me one."

She sighed and stepped back, and I was allowed inside her apartment. Sophie Kane's inner sanctum, where she was most herself and everything in the place reflected it. Bright green walls in the kitchen and soft gray in the living room. Shelves full of books, a great big TV. A big comfy couch and the beanbags on the colorful rug in the center of the room where she sat when she played video games.

I would sit halfway around the world with my own headset, sitting on some shitty chair in a green zone in the middle of the night, and play her, just so I could hear her voice for an hour.

"You want a drink?" she asked. "There's beer in the fridge."

"I'm all right," he said. "Open your present."

She opened the Tupperware and dumped the salad in a bowl. Checked the chicken potpie in the oven.

"You said I could yell at you."

"While you open it."

I shoved the box closer to her but she continued to ignore it and made herself another gin and tonic. A stiff one. The dead lime wedges from her previous drinks floating up from the bottom. Her face was stiff and I knew she was biting her tongue.

"Say it," I said.

She glared at me with so much heat. And I knew it was anger and she was right to be angry, but I also knew that underneath that anger she was wet for me. Just like I was hard for her. And I refused, refused to give in to it. But the longer she stared at me the harder it was to resist putting my hands on her. Sliding my fingers right into those shorts.

She swallowed like she was thinking the same damn thing.

"Just...say it," I said.

"We're not friends anymore," she said. I took the body blow and nodded. "I don't like you."

That wasn't totally true and I smiled, just a little, because I couldn't help it. Because she was mad and I was crazy for her when she was mad at me.

"Fuck you!" she snapped and stepped away from the kitchen island to walk past me toward the door, which she undoubtedly meant to throw open so she could kick me out. And...it happened again. My body, coiled and still and waiting, moved into action without my conscious thought. Without my brain processing the moment and commanding my body into motion, I was suddenly moving.

I put my hands on her, her elbows, and I spun her, rough, yeah, but not mean. Not hard. I heard the pull of her breath as I pressed her stomach into the island. I stepped up behind her, her body tiny against mine.

I was doing this. This was happening. Just like the other night. I was in the moment before my brain could even process the moment.

"You don't like me," I said into her ear, her hair brushing against my face, tiny little burns against my skin. I was hot in my coveralls, but they were protection against the heat of her. The *feel* of her.

"I don't," she said. So stiff against me. I felt myself smiling. The action before the thought. This wasn't safe. Everything could go sideways at any minute.

But I couldn't stop.

"But you like this," I said and slid my hand over the tender, sweet skin of her stomach, just above the waistband of those tiny, tiny shorts. "Don't you."

"No." Her voice was barely a breath and I could feel her tremble between my hand and my body.

"What will happen...?" I asked, my mouth at her ear, my teeth grazing her earlobe. She tasted like coconut shampoo and sweat. I wanted to eat her with a spoon. I wanted to strip her naked and feast on her skin, on her sweat, and every damp and delicious place on her body. And I wanted to do it for days. Years.

To make up for every second I'd been hungry for her over the years. To stock up for the lean years ahead when the taste of her was just a memory. "What will happen if I slip my hand..."

I put my palm over her pussy. Cupping the heat of her in my hand. I lifted and she was up on her toes, her ass pushed hard against my crotch. I groaned. And she made a sound in her throat. A moan she was swallowing.

"I want that sound," I said and put my mouth against her neck.

"Sam," she breathed.

"Give it to me." I squeezed her in my hand and the sound she made, that whimper/cry, that she swallowed. That she didn't want me to hear. "Or I can leave."

She was silent. So still. Waiting. And man, there was nothing I had respect for like waiting. Like stillness.

"Do you want me to leave?" I asked.

"Fuck you."

Yeah. I'd ruined everything. Even another chance at

having her like this. I closed my eyes and stepped away, my hand trailing from her body, and at the last possible second she grabbed me. My wrist in her strong grip.

"Don't—" She didn't finish the sentence.

"Don't what?"

Stop? Leave? Go? Stay? I had no idea what she was going to say. I held my breath. Waiting. Always, always waiting.

9

"Don't stop," she breathed and it was the gun at the start of a race. I was *on her.* I put one hand on her back, pressing her down on that island. Her ass, her perfect, perfect ass, peeking out from beneath that tiny tease of a pair of shorts. I unzipped my coveralls, letting them hang at my waist. The T-shirt I wore under it sweated through. I was so hot, so *on fire* for her, I was going to burn through my clothes.

I slipped my hand down the back of those shorts, pushing them down over her ass. She shifted like she was going to stand, and I kept my hand on the small of her back. Keeping her there, where I wanted her. The pink of that sweet skin between her legs, the cloud of pale hair. All of it. Exactly what I wanted.

"Stay," I whispered. "Stay right there." And I got back down on my knees behind her, pushed her legs out wide, and I licked her. and she jumped and squeaked and got so wet it began to drip down onto the skin of her thigh.

"Sam," she moaned.

"Yeah."

"Sam...I need..."

"What? Tell me."

"Here." She grabbed my hand, pressing my fingers down hard on her clit, and she was shaking. "Please."

I worked her hard, my tongue, my fingers. She came, screaming, and still I worked her. Wanting her boneless and limp. My fingers were slick and I pushed one inside her and she climbed the island, holding onto the far side for leverage as she fucked herself against my fingers and my face and loved it. I loved it all. I loved her abandon and her rawness. I loved how she came like she lived. All in. Dirty and sweet and all fucking in.

She was limp against the kitchen island, her thighs slick. The pink skin of her pussy twitching and damp. I licked her as I got to my feet, my knees creaking. My legs loose. I reached between my legs, my cock hard and dripping into my coveralls. I didn't want to think about it. I didn't want to count the days, weeks, months it had been since I'd managed to hold an erection and come.

The head wound. PTSD. The meds I was on...getting a hard-on was rare. Keeping it and coming was...not happening much any more. Except...Jesus...Sophie.

I wanted to come on her ass. Her tits. The small of her back. And I wanted to do it for the rest of my life. I stepped back again. Giving her room. Some distance.

"You okay?" I asked.

She stepped out of her shorts, wearing those pretty red socks and her favorite green Kane Co. sweatshirt. Her thighs were strong and lean. Freckled. I hadn't known that.

"Is this the part where you leave?" she asked, panting and flushed.

"Do you want me to?"

"I want you to stop asking me questions when I ask you

one," she snapped. Her cheeks pink. Flushed with sex and now anger. "Is this the part where you say something mean and leave?"

"I don't—"

"Is this where you make me feel used and cheap and—"

"Sophie. No."

"—stupid for letting you fuck me with your face?"

Oh. She wouldn't like it if I laughed at her. Even my smile was too much and she narrowed her eyes at me.

"Get out."

"Fuck you with my face?"

"What else would you call it? And get out!"

Yeah. I wasn't leaving. Not when she was wearing those socks and her hair was such madness around her head.

"I never meant for you to feel stupid."

"You told me you didn't want *this*." She waved her hands around her body.

"No." I stepped forward. My shirt was wet. The coveralls a furnace around my legs. "That's not what I meant."

"Well, it's what you said, and you don't get to change your mind just because you suddenly want to get fucked."

"You think I want to get fucked?" I asked, stepping closer to her.

"I think you're dreaming if you think you're going to fuck me."

I put my hand on her chest. Spread my fingers out wide and her pupils dilated. Her breath came fast. I could feel the pound of her heart through her clothes and my skin. The truth was on my lips—that this might all be big talk. That this might all be nothing. That I could be about to embarrass myself.

But I wanted *this*. I wanted *her*. I wanted to fucking try.

And because I'd been studying her. Because no one knew her like I did.

I put my hand around her throat. Holding her. Not hard. But...enough.

She started breathing harder. So did I.

"I didn't want to fuck you in the warehouse," I said. "I didn't want to fuck you when some other guy had been touching you and I didn't know if it was him you wanted or—"

"You," she breathed. "You stupid asshole. I lo—"

I kissed her. I kissed her to shut her up. I kissed her to keep her from saying something we couldn't walk away from. Something she might regret when this day was over. Something she might regret, depending on how the next ten minutes went.

She threw her arms around my neck and hopped, lifting her legs around my waist, climbing me like a monkey, and I walked her back over to the island, sliding her ass onto it. Pushing my cock, still hard, against her. The harsh fabric of my coveralls was too damn rough against her skin, but I wasn't going to stop long enough to take off my clothes when hers were a much bigger problem. I stripped off that sweatshirt, revealing a thin white camisole made of silk with a pretty lace edge. God, she killed me. It was so pretty. So feminine and sweet, and no one who saw her would ever call her that.

But I knew.

I knew her secret heart. Even without seeing it. Belief without proof was faith, and that was everything I felt for her.

I rubbed her nipples through the silk until they were hard beads against my thumbs. Until she was twisting against me. "Look at you," I breathed.

"Take off your shirt."

"I'm busy."

She grinned and then grabbed the bottom of my sweaty T-shirt, trying to pull it up over my head, but there was nothing that would change the direction of what was happening like her getting a look at my chest.

Too many scars, too many memories. Too many narrow misses and things that went wrong in a heartbeat. I'd lost weight. Too much. And between that and the scars, I looked like an animal. *Felt* like an animal.

The perfection of her touch suddenly felt like an itch, like something crawling under my skin, and I twitched away from her. Out of range. I closed my eyes and counted to five in the ten different languages I knew how to count to five in.

Breathe in.

Breathe out.

"Sam?" Her voice was quiet. Tentative.

"I'm okay," I said and opened my eyes.

There were a lot of crossed wires in my head. Things that didn't feel like they should. Emotions that got lost in translation and came out as anger. Touch that felt good, touch I craved, felt like something crawling under my skin.

It was hard to know what was true. But I felt naked. Exposed.

"Sam..." She hopped off the island and walked over to me, and I braced myself for her touching me. Braced myself for the terrible skin-crawling lie of her touch and blew out a sigh of relief of... bliss...when her touch was her touch. Exciting and sweet. A goddamn benediction when I'd never had one of those before. "Are you okay?"

"Sure."

"Do you want to leave your shirt on?"

"Sure."

"Does this hurt?" she asked, touching my ribs. My abs. Her fingers tracing the muscles under the damp T-shirt.

"No." The word came out soundless but she heard me. Felt me, maybe.

"Does it feel good?"

"Yes. But—"

I felt weirdly like a toddler in my shirt. Like a kid in front of a woman. This was why I should go, because the second act of this particular play was a real downer.

"No buts."

She unzipped my coveralls the rest of the way, the thick fabric falling off my hips and down my legs, and I stood there in my underwear. My cock was hard and she shoved down my thin boxers, damp with sweat, and she curled her hands around me. I gasped.

"Fuck, yes. Oh my God." The words exploded out of me despite all my misgivings.

She felt so good. So impossibly good.

I stepped out of the coveralls, pulling everything off my body except my shirt. I just wanted her and her hands. She put both hands around me, squeezing my balls, rubbing her thumb across the tip. I watched, mesmerized, breathless. Numb and dumb to everything but her touch.

And then she sank to her knees.

"No," I whispered. "Baby." I didn't know where that word sprang from but I tried to pull her back up. I'd been sweating and it didn't seem right—her on her knees.

"So help me God, Sam. If you don't let me suck your dick—"

The laughter barked out of me. Surprising. I mean...so fucking surprising. Like this woman who was grinning up at me, eyes sparkling, the devil in her grin.

Don't say it, I thought. *No good comes of you saying it.*

And I didn't. I didn't say it.

Even when her lips closed over the tip of my cock and it felt like I'd been struck by lightning, and she sucked me into her mouth and I could have died.

I love you. I love you so fucking much.

Because there was something weird in me. Profane. I cupped my hand around her head, taking this holy fucking moment and rubbing it in filth. "Suck me," I said. She moaned in her throat, her hand around my cock getting tighter, and she sucked me down until I felt the back of her throat with the head of my dick.

I put my fingers in her hair, the curls tangling around my fingers, and it must have hurt but I couldn't stop. I couldn't stop any of this. And I'd tried so long. I was weak against her. So weak. So powerless.

I felt the orgasm coming. I felt it in my balls. My back. My brain. I felt it in my gut.

With the only strength I had left against her, I pulled her to her feet. Her lips were pink and swollen; I crushed them under mine. I crushed her against me. The silk of her pussy. The perfection of it was my utter undoing. My total undoing. And she knew it, the beautiful bitch. She knew and she rocked herself against me. Fucked herself against me. I grabbed her ass with one hand, her hair with my other hand, and I came.

For the first time in so long, I came. Great mind-exploding bursts against her. On her. Some of it, undoubtedly, in her. And I couldn't be sorry. I couldn't be anything but out of my head with bliss.

When the storm passed, when it was all over, when it was just the two of us holding onto each other like the world was going to tear us apart, it was alarmingly...silent.

"You okay?" she asked, like she knew I was in over my head.

"Yeah. You?"

"A little...I'm, ah..." I leaned back and realized she hadn't come. Her hips were still shifting and rolling against mine, like she was searching for the right pressure. The pressure she needed. She was flushed and breathing hard. The camisole she wore was damp with our sweat, the cream silk transparent and her nipple was so pink. So hard and perfect. I put my mouth over it and sucked. Hard, because she was such a good girl and she liked that so much. I took the two steps back over to the island and set her down on it. She braced a hand behind her and I slipped my fingers down between us and slid two fingers inside of her. She was hot and wet and needed more, so I gave her a third and put my thumb down on her clit.

"Come for me," I said.

Her wide green eyes opened and locked on mine, and honestly, for a moment it was too much. The intimacy of this moment, of us, it nearly crushed me.

She grabbed my neck. My hair.

Her eyes on mine.

And she broke into a million pieces right in front of me.

10

S ophie

So. There was awkward. And then there was Fucking Sam Porter pulling his fingers out of my wet vagina and not looking me in the eye.

It was a whole new kind of awkward. An undiscovered flavor.

I flinched, pulling my legs together, and accidentally kicked him in the hip.

"Sorry."

"You okay?" he asked.

"Fine."

"Excuse me."

He stepped back and we both scrambled around for our clothes. I found myself not wanting to bend over in front of him, like the guy hadn't licked my asshole just a few minutes ago. And he put on his sweaty underwear when it had to be so uncomfortable. We couldn't even look at each other and I felt a little like crying.

How could something that felt so good, end up being so...awful when it was over?

"Sophie," he said, and I braced myself. Whatever was coming was going to be bad. I couldn't imagine him being mean—not after that. All that. My heart was still pounding. But I didn't know what he might say. "I never wanted you to feel used. Or stupid. I'm sorry."

I swallowed. Nodded. "Thanks."

Behind us the oven binged. The timer for the potpie going off.

In my shorts and sweatshirt I grabbed a tea towel, pulled out the chicken potpie, and set it on the burner on the stove.

"You want to stay for some food?" I asked, not sure if I wanted him to stay. Not sure if I could handle us being uncomfortable with each other.

"It's Christmas. I should go home. Mom, you know."

"Yeah. Of course."

"What are you going to do?" he asked.

Cry for a few minutes, I thought.

"Eat this chicken potpie. Drink some more gin and play video games."

"That sounds good," he said, smiling, and I smiled back, because it was basically our version of the perfect day.

He had his coveralls on but unbuttoned, and he reached into his pocket and pulled out a hat and his phone. I looked away, giving him some privacy as he checked his messages.

"My mom is actually going over for dinner at the neighbors'," he said.

He left that hanging there.

"Would you like to stay?"

Our eyes met and he was just my friend standing there.

And I loved him. I did. But that was all built on the fact that I loved him as a friend. And playing video games and drinking some gin with my friend did sound great.

"You got one of my shirts here?" he asked, shucking out of the coveralls.

"And some of your sweats, too."

"Let's do this. You go get my stuff and I'll make us drinks."

That's how I ended up spending Christmas Day with my brother's best friend.

And the love of my life.

Just waiting for my heart to get broken again.

Never say I'm not a sucker for punishment.

Sam

SHE GOT out the other beanbag and I found the controller I always called mine in the drawer of her entertainment center. We had icy cold G and Ts, my mom's potpie, and a couple of hours of finding magic scrolls ahead of us.

Any other time this would be one of the greatest days ever.

But what we'd done earlier made it...stiff. Awkward.

And I didn't know how to change that. So I sat there and ate the potpie and hoped, prayed, that Sophie had the grace to get us out this uncomfortable spot. Because I'd never had any grace.

"I don't know why I let you talk me into this game," she said as our characters walked through the woods toward the next challenge. "I swear, all we do is walk."

"And drink ale."

"It's like a video game of life."

"That's why I like it."

"I should have stuck with War Zone." She glanced my way, a small smile on her lips, and I felt the discomfort shift. Like a rock between us being rolled away. "Look what happens when I listen to you. I end up being an elf walking around a fake forest with a...whatever the hell you are."

"Mage."

"Wizard wannabe."

"Have I ever said thank you?"

"No. Never. Robbing me of hours of good times shooting bad guys."

"I couldn't shoot any more guys. Good, bad, or otherwise." I was surprised when the words came out of me. She looked at me, then looked back at the game as our mage and elf characters stepped into a pub to find the thief who had the directions to the castle. "So I was grateful when you agreed to play this. With me."

"Yeah," she said with a nod. Like it was no big deal, which was exactly what I needed from her. "No problem."

She stretched her legs out, the red socks and her freckled thighs distracting me for a second, and she got to the elf before me. "Are you home for a while?" she asked. "I mean, are you going back or...what?"

"Wes didn't tell you?"

"You told Wes before you told me?"

"It just...we were having beers a few weeks ago."

She stuck her tongue out at me.

"I'm out," I said. "I'm out of the Marines."

I was supposed to be saying that more. Out loud. I'd told Wes and I'd told my mom, but I hadn't told Sophie yet.

"For good?" she asked, staring at me, her mouth an O of surprise. The controller was forgotten in her hands.

"Come on, we're playing."

"Sam?"

"Yes. For good."

"You don't want to talk about it?" she asked.

"Do I ever?" I joked, but it wasn't really a joke. She was still looking at me and I knew I owed her more. More of an explanation. More conversation. But...things were so good right now and it was Christmas Day.

"Okay," she said quietly. "You're off the hook for the moment. Only because I'm dying to get to this castle."

I led us out of the pub and back onto the path. Walking some more. "I'll buy those directions off you." I was referring to what the thief had given her.

"You don't have any money."

"I have the sleep tonic."

"No way. You're not off-loading that bullshit sleep tonic—"

On the screen I threw the sleep tonic at her elf character, who immediately collapsed onto the dirt. I stole the directions and took off running.

"You are such a dick," she said and tossed down her controller. "You want another drink?"

I hesitated, thinking about Mom and the drive back.

"You can spend the night," she said. "No, you know, expectations."

Before the party I would have spent the night without thinking about it. I'd bunked down on her couch a million times. But now it seemed...weighted. Now the couch wasn't enough. I wanted into her room with all the pillows and the fancy sheets she treated herself too.

And I was weak. But I also didn't know how to say no to what I wanted. I'd lived in a state of denial for so long it was second nature. And suddenly, I just...couldn't.

"Sure," I said. "Another drink. I'll wait for you at the castle."

She walked away muttering and I adjusted my dick in my sweatpants, embarrassed by its sudden attention to detail. The flex of her knee, the curve of her thigh before it vanished into those sleep shorts. Yeah, my dick, lifeless for months, was suddenly noticing everything.

"So, you're staying," she said from the kitchen. Opening bottles, slicing limes. "In Denver?"

"Yeah."

"What are you going to do?"

I turned, looking at her in the kitchen, and she looked up and made eye contact with me. "What?" she said, and I could not believe that Wes hadn't told her. Though, the guy had had some other things on his mind.

"Wes gave me a job at Kane Co."

Her eyes narrowed. "Doing what?"

I grinned. "Working for you." She didn't look happy and I dropped my grin. "Is that a problem?" I honestly hadn't thought it would be a problem. I'd thought she'd...I don't know...look forward to having me around.

"No," she said, shaking her head. "Of course not. I'm... super happy to have you. You'll be great."

"But?"

"But...we can't...do that—" She waved her hand around the kitchen island where I'd all but fucked her. "Again."

Part of me wanted to shoot back, *Why not?* But I got it. She was the boss, I was the employee, and she had a hard enough time being a woman in charge of a bunch of men. I'd seen the way she handled those guys, and if some of them knew she was fucking another employee she'd never hear the end of it. I thought of Joe and how he'd made no effort to hide how much he wanted her.

"Yeah," I said. "I guess not."

I set down the controller. Got to my feet. Action before thought. And then I was in it, walking toward her, watching that smile illuminate her face, and I wouldn't have changed it if I could.

"You think you're gonna get one more in before I'm the boss of you?" she asked, cocking her hip. "You think you're gonna get that lucky?"

"I think you're going to get lucky," I said, coming right up to her, so tight. So close that when she took a breath her tits brushed my chest. I reached down and palmed her ass, fitting the tight globe of it into my hand. She opened her mouth to say something sassy and I smacked her ass, making her gasp, and then I crouched, put my shoulder in her stomach, and lifted her off her feet, making her squeal.

Her bedroom was dark and quiet, and by some unwritten rule, so were we. Silent, our hands over each other's bodies were careful and light. Like we were just finding our way in the dark. She pulled off my sweats, leaving my shirt. I pulled down her shorts and my fingers found her wet. So fucking willing.

Lying by her side, I curled one hand around the back of her neck, holding her still, and with the other hand I spread her wide open. Put one leg over my knees.

"Be still," I whispered to her face in the shadows. I could see the glimmer of her eyes and the curve of her cheek. I kissed her as softly and as sweetly as I'd always wanted to.

If I knew anything about her, she'd scoff at the idea of being cherished. But that's what I did. I cherished her. Her mouth, that sweet place between her legs. I made her arch and pant and beg.

"Sam," she whispered against my lips. "Please."

I shook my head because I only had *now*. I only had this.

And it had to keep me for a long, long time. But Sophie reached down and found my aching cock, wet from the come I could not control, leaking from the top.

This is so rare, I wanted to say to her. *This is so special. I never thought I would have this.* But I kissed her ferociously to keep those words inside my mouth. She jacked me like she knew just what I liked, but then I realized she was learning me the same way I was learning her. Paying attention to the way I arched into her hands. Moaned against her neck.

"Like that," she whispered, and I nodded, beyond words. So close to orgasm it was torture.

"Wait," she said, and I groaned, but lifted my fingers, wet from her body, to her stomach, where I felt the trembling of her muscles. "Is there a reason you're not fucking me?" she asked. "Like at the warehouse and earlier. Is this...all you want to do? Because that's cool, but if there's a chance I can get this cock inside—"

Action before thought. I rolled on top of her, shoving her knees out wide with mine, and I thrust so high and hard inside of her that she screamed, arching like a bow between me and the bed. "Oh fuck, yes. Yes!" she cried. Her fingernails deep in my back. Her legs a vice around my hips.

It was heaven. It was everything I'd never had the balls to imagine with Sophie. She fit me like no woman had ever fit me before. I gritted my teeth against the tide of my orgasm and braced my head against her chest.

"Fuck," she breathed. "What..." She thrust her hips, fucking me in shallow little motions that made my brain go blank. "What's wrong?"

"Nothing. Not one fucking thing." I took a deep breath, looked up into her glittering eyes. "Condoms?"

"I'm on the pill."

Oh sweet Jesus. Yes.

"I'm clean. Medically—"

"Me too."

And that was all I needed. On my knees, her hips in my hands. She braced herself against the headboard and I fucked her like I was dying. Like I was living. I fucked her until the orgasm was on me and I put my fingers against her clit, just the way I'd learned she'd liked, and she exploded. Her body a fist around my cock. Her body shaking and sweating. Everything so good. So perfect. A man like me didn't deserve this kind of moment. I didn't know what to do with it. How long I could hold on to it. What came after it?

My brain and the demons inside of it almost took this away from me, but I held on to her. Held on to Sophie.

I came, shaking and shuddering and grateful, against her. And when her hands came up to hold me, I'd never been so happy.

And I knew I never would again.

This was stolen time. A stolen Christmas. I could keep it but I'd never get another one.

11

S am

THE DREAM CAME like it always did. Noah, my spotter, my pain in the ass, the mouthpiece who, when shit hit the fan, is the steadiest goddamn hand I've ever known. We're lying flat on our stomachs in a gully so shallow it couldn't even be called a depression. He isn't wearing his ghillie suit, but a neon hat and gold chain necklace.

"What are you doing?" I ask, agitated, trying to keep my head down, my heart rate low. My voice nearly inaudible.

"You gotta loosen up," Noah says, practically yelling. Practically standing on his head. "We're fine."

"Get down."

"Sam. Whatever happened to your dad?"

"My dad?"

And then, in slow motion and from far away, I see the flash of a muzzle. "Get—"

And then Noah's head is in pieces and there's a burning pressure on my head and my skin....

"Sam!"

I jumped up, the dark cloying. Suffocating. I was cold and hot, and the worms were alive under my skin. A hand touched me in the dark and I smacked out at it. There was a muffled cry and a thump.

Stop. Breathe.

The dream vanished. Reality snapped back cold and hard.

"Oh, fuck, Sophie," I said. There was thin sunlight coming in through the curtains, the room not as dark as I'd thought it was. Proof that my dreams were so powerful that I couldn't see what was real and what was the misfiring of the chemicals in my brain. "Tell me you're okay."

"I'm okay," she said and turned on a lamp.

"I hit you."

"My hand. I'm fine. How are you?" She got up on her knees, naked and bathed in golden light. She reached for me, her fingers touching my arm, and I wanted it to be okay. I wanted it to feel like it should, like it had.

But it was all wrong. What was good was now terrible and I flinched away. And her face—her beautiful face—fell. And her hands jerked back and the room was suddenly cold.

"I'm..." A mess. Broken. Sorry. So fucking sorry.

"Yeah," she said. "Sure." She smiled as best she could and got off the bed. She grabbed the robe over a chair in the corner and pulled it over her body. Then she stood there, near the chair, pulling the tie around her waist tighter. "I'm going..." Away. Just away. She didn't say it, but that's what I heard.

"Okay."

And she was out that door so fast, and without the tension of her there I sat down on the edge of the bed and put my head in my hands.

Sophie

I went to the bathroom, and then to the kitchen to make coffee, because that was what I did every morning. I did it to keep my hands busy and to stall. I was stalling.

Stalling to figure out what to say.

How to say it.

Your mom told me...

Are you okay?

Can I help?

I want to help.

I love you so much. So much.

Sam came out, wearing the T-shirt he'd never taken off. His boxers. He didn't smile at me, just walked over to the beige heap of his coveralls and picked them up like he was going to pull them on.

"You're leaving," I said, sounding breathless and sad and I hated it.

"Yeah. Mom—"

"Right."

"Are you okay?"

"You didn't hit me." My wrist stung where his wrist bashed into mine. But he hadn't hit me. Not like he thought.

"It's the nightmares," he said, shaking his head. "They're..."

I waited to see how he could finish that sentence, how much he would tell me. How far he would let me in. It was crazy to me how deep we'd gotten with each other in the dark of my bed and on the kitchen island. But here, now, talking about what was wrong with him, what had happened, he gave me nothing. We were strangers.

It was like I'd given up our friendship when we became...whatever we were right now. Like we could be friends or we could be pseudo lovers but there was nothing in between.

Unless I fought for it.

"New?" I supplied, and he nodded, looking down at his feet. "Insomnia, too."

He looked up at me, his eyes sharp, and I nearly flinched. "Your mom...mentioned it. PTSD."

He started pulling on the coveralls, yanking them up his legs like they'd done something to upset him when I knew it was me that had upset him.

"Don't be mad at your mom."

"I'm not."

"Can you talk—"

He shook his head.

"Please don't leave like this," I whispered. "Even if we never..." I shook my head, swallowing the razor-sharp lump in my throat. "We're friends, aren't we?"

"We are, Sophie. We are friends." His voice was saying goodbye, the way he looked at me—all of it was goodbye. He glanced down at the kitchen island, like the imprint of our bodies was etched there by fire. "And it was amazing, Sophie. It was."

"I feel a *but* coming on."

"But I can't...give you that all the time. I can't even promise I can give it to you again. Half the time when someone touches me it feels...all wrong in my body."

"All wrong how?"

He opened his mouth, shut it. Shrugged, like he just didn't know what to say. How to explain it.

"That's what happened this morning?" I asked.

The morning light fell across his face, harsh and beautiful.

He was in so much pain. He was in pain from twenty

different things, in twenty different directions, and I couldn't stand, couldn't bear, that any of it was coming from me.

"It's okay," I said, and I put away all my own desires and wants. All my own pain, I put it down. Kicked it behind me into the corner. "We're friends. It was..." I couldn't finish that sentence. Didn't know how to.

"An amazing Christmas." He smiled at me, a real smile, and I felt joy looking at that smile. Glad I could give it to him. Even though it cost me everything I wanted. Everything I really wanted. "Sophie. You were so good."

"Well..." I winked at him. "You weren't so bad."

And it felt for a second like we were back to the place we'd started. Me wanting him so badly but locked in this friendship.

It had been enough for so long, I told myself, watching him zip up his coveralls. It will be enough again.

"I'll see you at work," he said.

"Yeah. Right." Oh God. Oh my God. Every day with him. Every day with this sliced-open feeling. Every day remembering how he touched me and then walked out that door. How in the world was I going to survive that?

He walked past me to the door and I reached for him, stupidly. Like a flinch nearly, like I had to stop him from leaving. I had to touch him one more time. Once more before he was gone and this weekend was just a memory with which I tortured myself.

But then I realized, reaching for him, that my touch wasn't comfort. That it might be the opposite of it. That I might actually be hurting him and I didn't know what to do with myself.

"Hey," he breathed, and he pulled me into his arms. A hug. Brief but hard, like the hugs he used to give me before we'd put our mouths on each other. And I held strong, forced myself not to melt into him. Not to soak him up. Not to lean and want and desire.

"See you at work," I said and slugged him in the shoulder.

And then he was gone.

I stood in my kitchen for a long, long time, trying not to cry. I lasted thirty second before I gave up, sat down on the floor, and cried until I was dry.

12

—————

S am

My first job out of the Marines. My first day. Two days after Christmas.

Mom had packed me a lunch. Turkey on rye. An apple. Some of that gingerbread.

Like I was ten.

I felt like a fool. And also...more than I'd thought, excited. Excited to be of use again. Particularly to Wes and Sophie. I mean, not that I had anything to add. I was just a warm body in the warehouse. But it felt good to be there. Among family.

Well, I hoped Sophie and I could feel like family again. I hoped I hadn't ruined that.

I walked in the front door, saw all the Christmas decorations still up. But then Kane Co. was a Christmas company and half the decorations were up all year round. But still, the wreaths and the lights were a reminder of the party. Of what happened between me and Soph.

But those reminders were everywhere for me. Sunlight coming in through the window reminded me of her. Half asleep this morning, my own hand on my own chest had felt like hers in my imagination and I got hard. Stayed hard. Put my hand around my cock and held onto the memory of her touch. Her lips. Her beautiful self.

Managed to come with a roar all over my stomach.

Don't think about it, I told myself walking into the warehouse. Don't think about her. Don't remember. The warehouse was quiet, though I could hear the hum of voices coming from what I knew was the employee break room. I walked down the hallway, past all the shelving and the packing section. The shipping desk.

Her desk. I didn't look at it or the floor in front of it, where her dress had pooled like a puddle of blue sequins.

Nope. I was all business.

Outside the break room was a crowd of men and women drinking coffee.

I found a spot near them, exchanged nods with a few of them I recognized, and looked inside the break room where Sophie stood, holding a meeting.

"You guys were amazing," she said, her eyes scanning the crowd. "We shipped sixty percent more ornaments than we have any other year. We streamlined all of our packing protocols. We saved this company about twenty thousand dollars this season. That's because of all of you." She started to clap, and around the room and in the hallway everyone was grinning. They loved her. Her spot in this family had always been unappreciated. She didn't have Wes's spark and drive, but she was a leader in her own way. Sparkly in her own way.

"We have inventory and cleanup for the next few days," she said. "And I'm open to all and any complaints about the season. Or recommendations to improve productivity or morale around here—come see me."

She made pointed eye contact with a couple of people and then clapped her hands. "But before you all get to work...you know what time it is."

There was a ripple of laughs and a few claps, and from a box on the table in front of her she pulled an ornament...

I tilted my head sideways.

"Is that what I think it is?" I asked.

"Naked Mrs. Claus ornament. It's a whole thing," said a woman standing next to me.

"The MVP of this year's holiday season is..." Sophie said, and staff at the table smacked the surface, creating a drum roll. "Joe Arben."

The handsome kid who'd had his hands on Sophie the night of the party, unzipping her dress with his mouth at her shoulder, stood up, all smiles.

"You assholes are never going to find it this year," he said and took the ornament from Sophie, then wrapped an arm around her waist and pulled her in for a hug. Which she accepted with a bright, merry laugh.

I turned, walking away from the break room into the main part of the warehouse just as Wes came through the big doors and stood on the landing at the top of the small staircase.

"There you are," he said with suspicious bonhomie. Not that he wouldn't be happy to see me. We were, after all, damn good friends, but this was a little...too happy.

The guy was getting laid. The marriage was real.

I could tell by looking at his face.

"You son of a bitch," I said, stopping in my tracks.

"Stop," Wes said, looking sheepish but still happy.

"Your sister is pissed." And hurt. But she wouldn't like me talking about that.

"My sister? About what, exactly?" Wes asked.

"About you getting for-real married without her being at the ceremony."

"Yeah," Wes said, stopping a foot away from me. "You're probably right."

"I'm pissed about it, too," I said.

"About not being at a wedding?"

"Not being best man. I figure I only have one shot at the job."

Wes smiled at me, and I recognized him as the kid I met on that basketball court, arguing with me over the free throw line. The kid who'd let me spend the night at his house when my dad was back. The kid who'd loaned me money so I could help bring my dad home, only so he could wreck it again. The kid who'd taken me aside and told me I couldn't steal things. That it would get me banned from the Kane house. From the Kane family.

And Wes didn't want me banned from the house. So I'd promised not to steal things.

I stole this Christmas with Sophie. I stole every kiss. Every touch. I stole the way she screamed my name and the way her body felt under mine.

I stole all of it, and if Wes knew about it, about me and Sophie, he'd...I don't know. Kill me? Be happy? I couldn't even guess.

"So?" I asked. "Everything good?"

"Yeah." He ran a hand over his head, that shit-eating grin in the corner of his mouth. "Real good. We'll talk, okay?"

"Yeah," I laughed. "We better."

"Hey." Wes stepped forward. "Your mom said your dad is sniffing back around."

"When in the world did you talk to my mom?"

"She called to congratulate me. She's always liked me best."

No, I thought. She always liked Sophie best.

"Is everything okay? With your dad?" Wes asked.

"He does this every holiday season," I said. "Gets nostalgic and kicked out of wherever he's been staying. Mom won't pull the trigger on a restraining order." Dad never got violent, just...pesky. And I could handle pesky. But the problem was what it did to Mom. She'd stopped letting him in years ago, but he still got in her head. Made a mess in her heart.

"Have you seen him?"

"No. He knows better than to show up when I'm around. And I'm around all the time, now."

"If you need anything..." Wes said, smacking me on the shoulder and I hid my flinch, shook out my hand. "I'm here."

"I know," I said.

"You get a tour or anything?"

"I know where the bathrooms are," I said.

"Hey." Wes stepped a little closer, dropped his voice. "You sure this is what you want? Working here?"

It was exactly what I wanted. "It's perfect."

"Well, you'll tell me if that changes, right? If you want to go, you don't owe us anything."

Oh man, that's where he was wrong. I owed Wes and Sophie everything.

But this job was good. Perfect.

Someone came running up from behind me and I turned, ready to put the person through a wall, but it was only that Joe kid who was so into Sophie. I still wanted to put him through a wall—but I curbed the action-before-thought instinct and just stepped out of the way. The kid, though, recognized me and stopped.

"You," he said.

"Joe," Wes stepped in. "Have you met my old friend Sam Porter?"

"Yeah," Joe said with his chin out, like he was going to pound his chest.

I smiled, which made Joe crazy, but I had no interest in fighting this kid. He'd tried to look after Sophie that night. Protect her.

"What are you always smiling about?" Joe asked.

"Hey!" Sophie came out of the break room, saw us all standing there, and came running. Everything she was feeling—happiness, anxiety, worry, a little bit of anger—it was all over her face, and swear to God, if she didn't get her poker face working, her brother was going to know something had happened between us without our saying a word. "Everyone...okay?"

"What's this guy doing here?" Joe asked, jerking his thumb at me, and I put my hands in my pockets, taking a step back.

"He's Sam," Sophie said. Like that explained it.

"And he works here now," Wes said.

"Newest member of the team," Sophie said with such brightness that even Wes looked at her out of the corner of his eye.

Joe made the most of his *I'm not sure of this guy* posturing, and then sucked his teeth and stepped back. "I gotta go hide this," Joe said, lifting the naked Mrs. Claus ornament.

"What exactly is the deal with naked Mrs. Claus?" I asked.

"We hide it," Sophie said. "Person who finds it hides it next and it…it's just a thing we do. You too, now," she said. "Since you work here."

"Sorry I forgot to tell you, Soph," Wes said. "About Sam working here. I figured it was fine, right? I mean, he's practically family, even though he's an asshole most of the time."

"It's fine," she said. "Good. It's great."

"I thought so, too," Wes said, turning for the door. "Okay, I'll let you get back to it. Oh!" He turned back. "Sophie, bring Sam on Thursday night."

"Yeah. Sure."

"Thursday?" I asked when Wes was gone.

"I go up to his office and we drink some of Dad's good scotch."

"Sounds like a good time."

She smiled, and again, her face revealed so much. So much of how she felt. And it was all…a lot. She felt a lot.

"Sophie," I breathed, a warning and…something else. Something I couldn't help but feel.

Regret.

And just like that her face was stone cold. Her eyes sharp. And all those feelings she felt for me were gone. Like she'd never felt them. And I felt regret about that, too.

"Come on," she said. "Let's introduce you around."

Sophie

· · ·

HE HAD A GOOD FIRST DAY. I made sure. I'd put Bob and Denise in charge of showing him around, and Sam and Bob and Denise had been laughing it up at lunch and in the back with packaging. I tried real hard to ignore them. To not be jealous when I heard him laughing, wondering what Denise or Bob said that made him laugh, and then wondering when I might have said something that made him laugh like that.

But I got myself back to work. I had a meeting in the New Year with W.B. regarding budget and costs, and I'd never been invited to one of those meetings. So maybe I was taking it too seriously? Hard to say, but I was prepping the big year-end report with color-coded tabs on my Excel spreadsheet.

But then I got to the fun part.

"Open for business!" I yelled from my desk, and the first person who came forward was Denise. The warehouse mom.

"You still want to do the Monday food swap?" I asked.

"Yeah," she said, pushing her glasses up higher on her face and glancing around. Some of the young guys were nodding. "I think it was a hit."

"What about trivia night?" Bob asked, leaning against my desk five minutes later.

"Friday night happy hour with trivia? You bet. But I'm inviting the glassblowers and sales."

There were groans and cheers, which was sort of how my ideas were received. But they loved it. And I loved it when they pretended they didn't. Affection shrouded in teasing was the only way I knew how to accept affection. It was a whole complicated thing. "Team sign-ups in the lunch room by the end of the day. I call teams with Alice!"

There were more shouts and groans, and I smiled down

at my computer. I had a few more tricks up my sleeve, and I was waiting for the quote from the new packaging supplier I was looking at for a pitch I was going to make my brother and W.B. on Thursday.

And I was keeping one eye on Sam, who was being put to work by Denise. During the months of October and November and December, it had felt like we were packing seven million hours into every day and one of the last things we were able to do was clean up. That was what January was for.

I also liked to use January to say thanks for everyone's hard work.

"What are you doing?" Joe asked as I hung up the new January lunch initiative in the break room.

"Getting organized. Putting up a new lunch initiative," Joe leaned over me to read the flyer. I shifted away from him. My skin had not grown back after my night with Sam. I was raw and uncertain in my body. Raw and uncertain in my warehouse, which I didn't like. Hadn't expected.

"Afternoon meditation?" he asked, like I had put up a flyer for afternoon decapitation.

"Yeah. The lunch room is going to be a quiet zone after lunch."

"What? Why?" he asked.

Because I'd done reading on PTSD and having a quiet place to go and then meditating at that place often helped with the anxiety associated with PTSD.

"What's this?" Joe asked, pointing to the other flyer.

"Morning run club," I said. Because I'd read that exercise helped, too.

"Is this for that guy? Sam?"

I glared at him hard. "No. It's for you and Denise and

everyone else who is working on New Year's resolutions to exercise more and reduce stress."

"Because you don't have to lose weight or whatever—"

"There are other reasons people run, Joe."

"In winter?"

"You don't have to do it," I cried.

I turned and he was standing there, looking me like he couldn't figure me out. "You okay?" he asked.

"Yes, Joe, I'm good."

"Because you were crying when you left the party. You were pretending not to, but you were crying."

Ah, Joe. He really was a sweet kid. I patted his shoulder, surprised he was still standing so firm in my corner. Surprised he was so solid under his sweatshirt. Man, the guy was working out somewhere.

"I'm fine," I said. "Don't you have work to do?"

Joe smiled and left, and I turned back around to put one more pushpin in my flyer. Maybe this was stupid—I mean, I couldn't guarantee anyone was going to do it, much less Sam. I couldn't guarantee Sam wouldn't see right through this and be pissed. But he was mine now. My employee. My guy in the warehouse and I took care of my people. I would be outside every morning ready to run.

For Sam.

Whether he was there or not.

Sam

As FAR AS first days went, this one hadn't been bad. Mostly taking down Christmas decorations and breaking down empty boxes. Denise was a good person. The staff worked hard, even on bullshit tasks. There was a serious team vibe.

And it was all because of Sophie.

All because of this...stuff she did.

Food swaps on Mondays when people brought in casseroles and homemade chicken wings and cakes, and everyone could fill up Tupperware containers and take them home for dinners or save them for lunches. Trivia night happy hours on Fridays.

And now meditation afternoons and morning runs.

I pushed my finger down on the thumbtack until I could recognize what I was feeling. Until it went from itchy to good to the hurt it was supposed to be. I just wanted things to feel the way they should. The way that made sense.

When all the physical feedback you got was messed up, it put you off balance. Made the whole world and your place in it feel unsafe. I didn't know what I could trust—not my body or surroundings, the ground under my feet.

But I knew *who* I could trust.

Sophie. Always.

She was doing that for me. The meditation and the running. Putting Denise on me.

For me.

After the weekend. Despite the weekend. I didn't know which one. Both? Sophie was a miracle.

"You coming?" Denise stuck her head into the break room and I pulled my finger back from the thumbtack. She and some of the rest of the warehouse crew were taking me out for a drink. Sophie, I'd noticed, because I noticed everything about her, had taken off early, saying she had to do some work on a budget pitch she had for her brother.

But I knew she was stepping away in part so I could... bond or whatever with the staff. Or maybe, and probably more likely, she was just uncomfortable around me. The same way I was uncomfortable around her.

This was why I'd stayed away all those years. *This* was what I was scared of.

Ruining what we had.

If she was going to do this for me, I had to do something for her. Move her past me.

Past us.

13

———

S^{am}

WHEN I'D WOKEN up in Landstuhl—the military hospital in Germany—I'd moved my arms and legs and wiggled my toes. Checked my junk and been able to remember my name. I'd known, of course, my career was over. I didn't have any more ambushes left in me. I wasn't going to lose another spotter. Another friend. My nerve was gone; I felt its absence in my gut. I felt the vacuum where my duty and my will to serve and my sterling belief that I was on the side of angels had been.

I was now former Marine. And once I'd come to grips with that, the next thing I'd thought was, *Thank God I don't have to run anymore.*

Which didn't explain even a little bit why I was standing outside the Kane Co. building in a sweatshirt and a hat getting ready to go running.

With Sophie.

She came out the front door wearing black running tights, a sweatshirt, and gloves. Her curls were in a ponytail.

"Hey!" she said, unable to hide how delighted she was to see me. She beamed in my direction, and if there'd been anyone else there they'd have seen it on her face.

How much she loved me.

Don't, I wanted to say to her. *Don't look at me.*

Don't love me.

I looked into the gray skies and stomped my feet against the cold.

"Where is everyone?" she asked.

"There is no everyone," I said. "Just me."

"You want to scrap running and go get some pancakes?" she asked. Now her face was all love and hope for pancakes.

"No," I said. "But you go ahead if you want pancakes. I'm going to run."

"Then I'll run with you," she said, still bright and cheerful. And I hated the idea of being cruel to her, but she had to stop looking at me like that. I had to *stop* her from looking at me like that.

I took off running, a steady trot away from the building, down through LoDo toward the river.

"How was your first day?" she asked, catching up with me.

"Fine."

"Denise—?"

"She's nice," I said, turning left to catch a green light so we didn't have to stop at a corner.

"The rest of the guys?"

"Fine." We caught the next red and I stopped running and she jogged lightly.

"Great," she said brightly. "How is your mom?"

I smiled at the change of subject. "Fine. Good." I shook my head because that was a lie.

"What's wrong?" she asked.

"Nothing...new."

"Your dad?"

I nodded and she stumbled.

"He's around?"

"He just called, but you know how that goes."

"Is he in town?"

"Apparently. His last girlfriend kicked him out."

"Have you seen him?"

I shot her a look. "He knows better."

"What can I do?" she asked.

"I got it," I told her, unhappy with myself that I'd told her. But man, it was hard living without friends when your asshole dad showed back up to make your mother cry. "But there is something else you can do for me."

"Name it."

"Go out with that Joe kid," I said, and the light changed and I started running and she was caught flat-footed.

"Joe?" she said when she caught up.

"Yeah. He's into you. Seems like a good enough guy."

This time when she stopped it was the center of the street with the walking timer clicking down. She pursed her lips at me, hands on hips. "Good enough was a nice touch," she said. I stood on the curb and held my arms at my sides.

"He seems into you."

"Oh, he's really into me. You're going to pretend like you don't care?"

She was standing in the middle of the road when the light changed. There were cars coming down the road right at her and she stood there, pissed off and trying to piss me off.

I ran into the middle of the road and grabbed her by the arm and pulled her over to the side. "I don't care," I told her pink cheeks and fiery eyes.

"What bullshit," she said.

"I'm not lying."

I was thankful, so thankful. And deeply amazed at how lucky I was to have Wes and Sophie as friends, but...there was a limit. There had to be one. Otherwise I was just some object of pity and need who didn't have a job and couldn't sleep and wanted to kiss my best friend's little sister until this hunger I had for her was gone.

But it would never be gone. So I couldn't even start because, in the end, I was just an object of pity and need who didn't have a job and couldn't sleep.

And I didn't want to be that guy, that sad sack. But Sophie deserved better than a guy who sometimes didn't feel good when he was touched. Whose dad was showing up out of the murk where he lived.

I got down into her face, close enough to feel her warm breath on my cold cheek. I could smell the coffee she drank and the mouthwash she used beneath that. If we'd been different people...no, I had to be honest in this moment. Every moment. I couldn't afford to be otherwise. If I were different...if I were different we might have had a chance.

But that was a daydream I couldn't afford.

"Go out with Joe," I said.

And then I turned and ran away, leaving her behind.

Sophie

· · ·

I AVOIDED HIM. It was easy. The warehouse was big and he was avoiding me, too. I saw him every once in a while, answering his cell phone and then hanging up. And I wondered if it was his father. And then told myself it wasn't any of my business.

We went two days without seeing much of each other. I didn't show up to run anymore, but the afternoon meditation was a hit, though I think people were just closing their eyes for a half hour.

But I saw Sam going in there every day and I wanted to call his mom and tell him he was trying. Or at least pretending to.

"So?" Joe asked, leaning up against my desk where I was putting the finishing touches on what I was going to pitch to my brother during our Thursday night drinks.

"So what?" I asked, trying to figure out the equation for a spreadsheet cell.

"You gonna come with me?" he asked.

"Where?"

The entire row of numbers vanished on my spreadsheet. "Crap!"

"Sophie."

"No. I told you," I said, quickly trying to undo everything I'd done and then I'd undone too much and I had an extra row.

"You said you were thinking about it."

I sighed and looked up at him. "Joe. You are...sweet but I gotta tell you, it's never going to happen."

"You're not going to come to a New Year's Eve party with me?"

I shook my head.

"Your loss," he said.

New Year's Eve was the next night, staff had that afternoon off, and then it was the weekend. And I was going to pitch my idea to my brother tonight, come in tomorrow for the potluck, and then I was going to hide in my apartment for a while and talk myself out of my feelings for Sam.

I had a whole plan. Count all the terrible things about him. Remember in excruciating detail everything he'd ever said or done that hurt me. If I focused hard enough, I was pretty sure I could pull these feelings out by the roots.

He'd been ignoring me. No, that wasn't totally true. He'd been treating me like I was a boss. Listening at meetings. Working hard. Saying thank-you and asking questions. Respectful and decent. He'd been treating me like nothing had happened between us.

In fact, he was so good at it, there were seconds after he came in, in the morning, after giving me his blank smile and cool eyes, that I actually wondered if I'd made it up somehow. Like it was a fever dream.

At night, when I got home and ate my burrito, took my hair out of my ponytail, and fired up my PlayStation...there he'd be. Not in real life, obviously. But his stupid wizard wannabe character, with his dumb face and his map.

Castle is waiting, he'd message me. I'd look at his name on my screen and I'd feel the loss of him in the pit of my stomach. And he was right there.

I didn't know how he could turn it off like that. And staring up at my ceiling at night, the only thing I could think was that it just didn't mean anything to him. That *I* didn't mean anything. And I tried, I really did, to pretend that he didn't mean anything either.

But every time he looked right through me, it hurt. And every time he walked into the room, it hurt.

So I had New Year's Eve and the weekend to burn him out of my head.

I couldn't even fire him. He was a hard worker and people liked him and he was a vet with PTSD and I wasn't an asshole.

But it hurt. Everything hurt when it came to Sam Porter.

Thursday night the warehouse emptied out quickly and I printed off the last of my stuff to take up to talk to my brother. A soft pitch before going to the board, W.B., and my mother. But I was still nervous. There hadn't been a lot of ideas coming from me during this whole Kane Co. fiasco. Partly because I ran the warehouse and partly because my father didn't like it when other people had ideas and partly because...my family never looked to me for ideas. Wes was the ideas man.

"Hey."

I jumped, pulling the papers out of the printer with a jerk so they scattered across the floor. Of course it was Sam standing there in his hoodie and dark jeans.

I grabbed the papers before he could because I didn't want him to see them.

"What's..."

He had a paper in his hand and I grabbed it.

"Sophie?"

"What."

"You okay?"

"Fine. You leaving?"

"I thought..." He paused and blinked at me. Which, in Sam Porter language, was a whole thing. A whole conversation, and because I was fluent in Sam Porter language I knew that he was thinking, *I thought we were both going up. Did you forget? Did I forget? Do you not want me to be there? That's it. Okay. I won't go.*

"Good night," he said and started to walk toward the door, and the crazy thing was the guy broke my heart but I was never able to hurt him. I was never able to see him hurt. It hurt too much.

So stupid. So much stupid.

"I'll be upstairs in a little bit," I said. "You know where Wes's office is?"

"Sure," he said, glancing down at the papers in my hand. "I can wait for you."

"I don't want you to," I said, and it was snappy and mean because I didn't know how to talk to him without using that voice. Everything that had been easy between us was broken now. "I'm just...working on something."

"You've been working on this something for a while."

He'd noticed. Of course he'd noticed.

"A few months."

"The last few days quite a bit," he said, and I felt like a rabbit in a field with something hunting me. "What is it?"

I was really nervous. I was nervous about talking to my brother. I was nervous about being wrong. About being told that I was stupid. That maybe I *was* stupid.

"Nothing," I said and put the papers in a stack.

"Sophie—"

"It's a cost thing. We lose money to breakage, and I think if we upgrade our packaging we'll save money. But the packaging costs more than what we usually spend. I want to pitch it to my brother."

"Well, you sold me."

"I think you're an easy sale."

There was a joke there about how he was just easy. Or maybe I was the easy one and I wanted to make it, but swallowed it back.

"I'll see you up there," he said and he left.

· · ·

Sam

"HEY!" Wes cried as I came in the door. He had his feet up on his father's old desk. The whole office was a bit of a throwback to some kind of *Mad Men* situation. There was the big desk and a leather couch. But his father had never allowed any Christmas decorations in the office, so in true Wes style, Wes had put up lights and an obnoxious light-up Santa on the wall. When he pressed a button, Santa would dance, sing "Jingle Bells," and say "Ho ho holidays!" in a way that would give anyone nightmares. Wes got a satisfied smile on his face every time he pressed that button.

"You know," Sam said as he went in. "I know you hate your dad and all, but you can take that Santa down anytime."

"Now you've hurt Santa's feelings," Wes said. "He's going to haunt you for that. Where's Soph?"

"On her way." I thought about maybe saying something about how nervous she was but she would not appreciate me getting in the middle of her and her job.

"How... how is she doing?" Wes asked.

"You can ask her in ten minutes."

"Yeah, but has she been weird? With you or anything?"

Weird? That was one way to put it. But Wes didn't really want to know everything going on between me and Soph. "She's been good. Busy. She runs a tight ship down there."

Wes pursed his lips and nodded. "She's been giving me the cold shoulder."

Oh, I thought, Wes had no idea what kind of cold shoulder Sophie could give. We were stumbling over snowbanks down there in the warehouse, me and Soph. Ignoring each other in a way that made the ice climb the walls. And then we'd catch each other's eyes and the heat that flared turned it all to steam. It was so obvious I'd caught Denise staring at me a few times.

We were a mess down there, and I'd made it that way. The only thing that would make it better was leaving and it was the one thing I could not do.

"So, what are you drinking?" Wes asked as I sat down in one of the swanky leather club chairs in front of the desk. Wes opened up the liquor cabinet and it was like a cave of wonders in there. Booze covered in dust. Booze that looked like it had been bottled by monks a hundred years ago. Some of those bottles cost hundreds of dollars, and there were a lot of them.

"The company was going down the gutter and your dad was drinking top shelf booze?"

"What can I say? He's an asshole. And a lot of this stuff might be top shelf, but it tastes like garbage. Once Sophie and I drink all of this, I'm throwing out this cabinet." He looked at the bottle in his hand. "What kind of throwback has a liquor cabinet in his office, anyway?"

"The kind who embezzles money, I guess."

Wes grinned at me. "Look, I'm making the choice. You're drinking scotch."

"Perfect."

My old friend sat back down with a sigh and splashed very old, very good scotch into two gold-rimmed glasses. Honestly, when I thought about Sophie and her casseroles and the potlucks and the trivia nights, I thought for the millionth time that their father did not deserve his kids.

"So," I said sipping my scotch. "I take it you're not getting divorced, as planned."

His smile made me pause, the glass halfway to my mouth. I'd seen my friend drunk for the first time and I'd seen him the first night he got laid, and I'd seen him the night his father got arrested for embezzlement, but I'd never seen him like this. Happy. Like someone had put a lightbulb up his butt. "Nope. No divorce, though thanks for the idea. We're staying married. I'm telling you man, my parents, your parents, no one gave us any idea how good it could be."

"What?"

"Love. Marriage."

"I imagine it's the love that makes it good. And our parents never had that."

"Your dad still sniffing around?"

"A little. He'll get bored and leave soon enough."

"Your mom?"

"Rattled, but resolute. I keep telling her to get a restraining order."

"Oh, man," Wes said. "I'm sorry."

I raised my scotch in a mock salute. "Dads. What are you gonna do?"

"Well, mine's going to jail and it's not half bad," Wes said, and suddenly we were laughing like we used to and it all felt pretty good.

"That's a sound I haven't heard for a long time," Sophie said, coming into the office like a whirlwind. "You two laughing."

I gave myself a second to take her in, to soak her in and hold her for just a second, and then I buried my face in my scotch glass.

"Wes is very funny," I said.

"No, he's not," Sophie said with a big wide smile.

"I'm sitting right here. Scotch?" Wes asked his sister.

"Gross. Is there any of that bourbon from last time?"

"You drank the last bottle."

"Rats. How about that red wine?"

"I took it home to Penny. She likes red."

Oh, Sophie was so quietly hurt. So carefully trying not to show her brother that she was. "She should come to these Thursday nights."

"She had some work to do. But...we were hoping you'd come spend New Year's with us. Both of you." Wes pointed his finger at me. "And don't say you can't."

"Why not?"

"Because you'll be lying and you shouldn't do that to your only friends."

Sophie laughed. "I'll be there," she said. "But I expect you to feed me. Something good. Expensive. Like the kind of food I'd be served at a wedding."

"I will," Wes said. "And I'm sorry. It just happened. We went to City Hall, and—well, I'll tell you the whole story if you get me drunk enough. We're talking about doing a thing in the summer."

"A thing with dancing? Speeches?" she asked, her eyes narrowed.

"You will have your moment to publicly embarrass me. Both of you."

"I get to tell the story of him falling asleep on the BART in San Francisco," Sophie said, smiling at me.

"That's fine. I have the one of him getting nailed in the junk by Annabeth—"

"All right. I can already tell this is a huge mistake. So?" he said, looking between us. "New Year's Eve. Steaks. Booze. Cheesecake. Some auld lang syne."

I was trying not to get myself any more tangled up with Sophie, but there was no way to say no. "Of course, man."

There was another knock on the door and suddenly W.B. was standing there. I'd met him a few times. Good guy. I'd had a sergeant like him on my first tour; he thought he could control the world with meetings and plans and discipline. But the world loved to turn that kind of guy on his head. There were rumors that W.B. had been turned on his head by the beautiful glass artist who'd been hired to create new ornaments.

"W.B.," Wes said. "Come on in and have a drink."

"Well," he said, eyeing the drinks and the chairs as if he was running a cost–benefit analysis on all of it. "I suppose one won't hurt."

"What's your poison?" Wes asked. "There's a rare vodka in the back that my dad got from someone he was laundering money for. There's a plum schnapps from who knows where and this scotch that probably cost—"

"Three hundred dollars a bottle," W.B. supplied.

"Yeah." Wes shrugged. "We both know Dad liked to spend money he didn't have. My plan is to drink every drop. It might take a while, but I'm committed."

"Do you have a beer?" W.B. asked.

"Sure," Wes said, pulling open the mini fridge and handing WB a bottle of beer.

"I want one of those too," Sophie said, putting down her glass of very expensive scotch.

Wes handed her one and looked at me. I waved him off. I would drink the expensive scotch because that was what I'd been given.

"So," W.B. said. "I wanted to hand you the final reports for the year and talk about projections for next year."

"Well, on Thursday I drink with my sister. You can leave the reports and we can schedule a meeting for the New Year."

"Sophie should be at that meeting," I said and took a sip of my scotch, letting it burn down my throat even as Sophie's pissed-off gaze burned the left side of my face.

"She is," W.B. said.

"I am." Sophie nodded.

"You are?" Wes asked clearly this was all news to him.

"She's got an idea. A plan," I said and gestured to the papers in her hand.

"It's..." She sighed. "It's about the packaging."

"Well!" a new voice said from the open doorway, and in front of my eyes Sophie wilted as her mother came into the room. "I can't get either one of you to return my calls or come to my house for a holiday, but here you are."

14

———

It was like the room just went flat. And cold. God, this woman was the worst.

"Hello Mom," Wes said, getting to his feet to kiss Gloria Kane primly on each cheek.

"Where's your wife?" she asked, smiling slightly at her son. "Or did you use the card I gave you?"

Wes's face went hard and still. "Mom, this isn't the best time."

"Well, I don't know when the best time is for anything anymore," she said with a brittle shrug. There was a silence in the room, the kind of silence that happens just before a firefight. Everyone holding their breath, wondering if Gloria was a grenade with a pulled pin.

"Penny is working," Wes said.

"Well, I would think you'd put a stop to that."

"Mom—"

"It being a holiday and everything," she said quickly, but what she'd really meant was clear. Clear on her face and the way she'd lived her whole life in her husband's mealy shadow. I stood and touched Sophie on the shoulder and gestured for her to take my seat, then I stood in the corner.

"Mom," Sophie said, leading her mother to her chair where the two of them shared a cool hug. Over Sophie's shoulder, Gloria caught my eye and stiffened.

"I didn't realize you were still in town," she said to me.

"He works here now, Mom," Sophie said.

There had been so many times in my brushes with Gloria Kane when her looks, if they'd had the power, would have had me dead and buried. But this look she was giving me—it was nuclear. I'd have been dead and buried—and so would everyone within a three-mile radius of me.

It was another reason Sophie and I were a bad idea. The cold relationship she had with her mother would literally freeze over and shatter. And maybe that would be all right for Sophie, but it wasn't up to me to make that decision.

"Mom, would you like a drink?"

"Is your father's vodka still in there?" she asked, and I caught Sophie's eye roll and worked very hard not to smile.

Wes poured his mother a drink and W.B. leaned forward, his beer half gone. "Sophie," he said. "Do you want to finish what you were saying? Your plan?"

"Sophie has a plan?" Gloria asked. "For what?"

Oh God, this was...bad. Sophie was nervous about it already and would never put herself out there in front of her mother.

"Nothing," Sophie said stiffly.

"Well, I don't mean to interrupt," Gloria said, like there was a stiffness competition.

"If you have an idea," W.B. said, opening up his folders. "I'd love to hear about it. I know we haven't worked together closely in the past, Sophie, but when it comes to saving money, any idea is a good idea."

Gloria cleared her throat. Not a scoff, really. But not...not a scoff.

"Here," Sophie said and pushed the papers she'd been twisting her hands. "You can look at it. It's probably nothing—"

"You lost money to breakage," I said, unable to keep my mouth shut. Unable to watch Sophie shrink in her chair when she should be proud of her ideas. And maybe I wanted to give her mother the finger. "She has a plan to help."

"Packaging," W.B. said, like the word had just occurred to him.

"It...it costs a little more," Sophie said. "But in the long run..."

"I do love the long run," W.B. said as he started to look through the papers.

"W.B., have you met my mother?" Wes asked.

"I don't think so," Gloria said.

"A few times, actually," W.B. said, and he stood and shook Gloria's hand. I was happy to see she gave him the same limp-wristed shake she always gave me. At least that part wasn't personal.

W.B. sat back down, his attention on the forms Sophie'd handed him.

Gloria turned my way. "You're out of the army?"

"Marine Corps," I corrected her for the hundredth time. "And yes."

"And you're working here now?" she asked.

"Yes, ma'am."

"That's convenient, isn't it?" It was one of her questions that had a thousand different meanings, all of them with an edge of meanness, and I always wondered if it was because I was poor. Or because Wes and Sophie so clearly loved me when they weren't always fond of her. Or perhaps it was just living in the shadow of her husband, who'd been cruel and suspicious. It had to get cold there. And lonely.

There were times I wondered what would have happened to me without Wes and Sophie. Without their affection and loyalty and trust. My father's shadow was real cold and lonely, too.

It wasn't always easy to have compassion for Gloria Kane, but sometimes I managed to muster some up.

"For us," Sophie said. She had that look in her eye. Fight mode engaged. I loved that look. It was my second favorite of her looks. The first was fuck mode. But that was new and I wasn't planning on seeing it again. I wanted to put my hand on her shoulder, tell her it was all right. Tell her I had thick skin and that I didn't need her to battle for me. "Mom, it's lucky for us," she said, all prickly. Completely in my corner with her teeth bared.

Yeah, I couldn't quite pull myself back from the urge to brush my fingers across the back of her hand where it sat on the arm of the chair. I did it and she glanced back at me in that painfully Sophie way, and that was what her mother saw.

"Lucky for you," Gloria said to her daughter. "He's why you suddenly have cost-saving ideas. Why you're writing reports. Wearing dresses and doing something with your hair. This boy always went right to your head and—"

"Stop," I said. My voice boomed in the office. I stood up from where I'd been leaning against the windowsill. The room went still and W.B. slowly closed his file. I could see him trying to shrink back into the shadows. "When you talk to Sophie like that all you do is prove how little you know her."

I felt the attention of everyone in the room. Except Sophie. Sophie, who was decidedly not looking at me.

"Thanks for the drink," Sophie said, draining the last of her beer and getting out of that office as fast as she could. While I stood there, paralyzed. Hating that I'd said that, but also knowing I would have hated it had I kept my mouth shut. I'd done it my whole life with Gloria Kane and if I was here now, well, I couldn't keep doing it.

Sophie deserved better.

W.B. quietly left the room.

"You think you know my daughter better than me?" Gloria asked. She got to her feet. "You came to our house with nothing and my kids took care of you, and I know you all think that I've been cruel or mean towards you but it is because you have been rude in every single exchange we've ever had. You—"

"Mom!" Wes snapped getting to his feet.

Gloria, to my shock, got right in my face. "They loved you. My children. Sophie, especially. You'd have to be dumb or blind not to see that. And you joined the Marines like their love meant nothing. You could have died and she...." Gloria took a deep breath and stopped.

"That's why you don't like me?" I asked, stunned.

"No. I don't like you because I don't like you."

For some reason the honesty of it all made me laugh. Which, predictably, made her sniff and set down her vodka on the edge of the desk. She turned to Wes. "You got married without even telling me."

"Mom." Wes sighed. "There were reasons. We didn't tell anyone—"

"I'm not anyone. I'm your mother."

Wes nodded, taking that little jab on his chin, and she

turned her mean eyes back my way. "Don't you hurt her," she said, and then she, too, was gone.

"What are you doing with my sister?" Wes asked into the long silence after his mother left, and I thought about saying something. I thought...about telling him. Not that something had happened but that something might.

Could.

Will.

"Nothing," I said.

"Oh my God, what bullshit." Wes laughed and I looked up at him. "Man, there has been something between you forever. I try to ignore it because I don't like to think about it, but I'm not stupid. The first year you came back and you couldn't tell us where you'd been, remember? That spring?"

"No."

"Sure, buddy. You keep saying that. I'll remember for you. Sophie had turned twenty and I saw your face when she got out of the truck."

I looked away, out the dark window with snow melting against it.

"I saw your face," Wes said. "And for once, and I mean once, I knew exactly what you were thinking."

I remembered that moment, her getting out of the truck in a pair of cutoffs and a smile. The rest of it...

"I don't remember," I said.

"Sophie? That day? What—"

"Knowing what I was thinking." I said it and cringed. I wasn't making sense and I shook my head. "Ignore me."

Wes got up and walked around the desk, and I braced myself in case he was going to put a hand on my shoulder. But he didn't. My oldest, dearest friend in the world understood my boundaries and leaned back against his desk.

"I like you two together," he said, surprising me. "I

always have. I mean, who doesn't want his best friend at every family function? Christmas parties, backyard barbecues, raising our kids together—"

"Stop."

"Sam. I'm telling you, you have my permission. My blessing. Whatever. But..."

"But?"

He stood up from the desk, pushed through that boundary. I tensed. "Right now, you're hurting her. I don't know what you did. Or what you're doing. But you're hurting her and you keep doing that and...you and me?"

I saw that kid on the basketball court, arguing with me about the free throw line. The one who told me not to steal from his family again. That he would help—anything I needed—but I had to ask.

"You and me will be over, Sam. I love you like a brother, but she's my sister and you keep hurting her and you're out in the cold."

I was already out in the cold, I thought. Already living there. And this family... goddamn it, this family kept asking me in.

"I...tried not to hurt her," I told him. Which was the truth and not the truth. The last few days in the warehouse, pushing her away, I'd hurt her.

"Well, you fucked it up. I suggest you figure your shit out. Quick. Because I don't like seeing my sister look like she's been punched in the gut."

Neither did I.

"You wouldn't...care?"

"The two of you?" Wes shook his head. "I'd love it. I mean...I don't need details, but I'd love it. Wouldn't you?"

15

———

S ophie

WHO GETS mad at a guy for saying something nice? For saying something really true? For defending me to my worst critic? My mom. Being angry at Sam didn't feel right, but it wasn't like I could stop it.

There was so much about Sam I just couldn't stop.

I couldn't stop being friends with him. I couldn't stop loving him.

Which was why I was standing in the freezing cold in front of his truck in the parking lot, because I couldn't do anything without him.

It didn't take long. He'd had his coat and hat with him in Wes's office and he wasn't one to linger. Mom had left a few minutes ago, her big old Cadillac easing out of the parking lot, her taillights heading in the direction of home.

The lights were still on in Wes's office, and as I watched,

the lights blinked on in W.B.'s office and then blinked off, and then, suddenly, there was Sam, shoulders hunched against the wind and the snow, looking like a bull coming through the lights around the parking area.

"Hey!" I said when he was close enough.

"Soph."

"Yeah. What was that in there? With my mom? With W.B.? What were you doing?"

"Nothing, Sophie—"

"No. It wasn't nothing. It wasn't...what were you doing?"

He was quiet. Still. His jaw hard as a rock. He turned to stare at his truck, but that was an old trick of his and I swept snow off the hood, packed it into a ball, and threw it at him. And I don't mean to brag, but my aim was excellent and I got him right on the shoulder. The snow exploded up onto his chin.

His eyes went wide and I refused to smile. He reached for snow off the back of his truck, but I was faster and got him again. My snowball hit him square in the chest.

"Sophie!"

"You can't have it both ways, Sam!" I snapped. Hot with my anger and everything I'd been swallowing and pretending for the last week. "You can't be my friend and ignore me. You can't defend me to my mother and pretend I mean nothing to you. You can't—"

He rushed me. *Rushed* me, and I retreated, slipping on the ice, and suddenly my back was against the truck and he was pressing me there with his body.

His hands were holding my face and all I could feel was him and the pound of my heart.

"I have been trying to ignore you," he said, and I shoved at him. "But you are impossible to ignore."

I would not be melted by those words. Nope. I was

furious and righteous, and pretty words from Fucking Sam Porter meant nothing to me.

"And you mean everything to me," he said, and if I could resist pretty words I could not...could not resist his kiss. It was too new. Too sweet.

He held my head and kissed me and I melted. I melted as fast and as completely as the snow caught in between his coat and the warmth of his skin. His tongue brushed mine and the smell of him was my entire world. He was my entire world. And I felt myself opening up to him. Opening everything up to him. My mouth. My heart.

"You threw a snowball at me," he said, kissing my lips. My cheek. I felt myself smiling, despite not wanting to smile at all.

"I'm not sorry."

"Of course you're not."

He sighed and leaned back, away from me. But his body was still pressed to mine, keeping me sandwiched between his heat and the cold steel of his truck.

"You asked me to date some other guy," I whispered. "Do you really want me to do that?"

I felt his phone ringing in his pocket and he blinked, but didn't answer it. It rang again. And then again.

"I have to get that," he said.

"Sure."

"I mean my dad is around and Mom—"

"Answer the phone, Sam."

He fished it out of his pants and pressed the screen with his thumb.

"Mom?" He turned sideways. "Mom. Calm...okay. Okay... I'm...crap...okay. Mom, I'll be there soon. I'm coming right now. No! No. Listen. Do not let him in. Call the cops." He sighed, his head in his hand. "Okay. I know. But...just don't let him in."

He hung up and turned. "I gotta—"

"Is she okay?"

"No. My dad is drunk and outside, and she's just..."

"I'm coming with you. I'll follow. You handle your dad and I'll help your mom."

"Sophie, you don't have to do that."

"Sam. You and me are super fucked up right now, but your mom is family to me and you know that."

"Thank you," he said, and I wanted to kiss him. I did. Because I'd never in my life seen a guy who needed to be kissed as much as Fucking Sam Porter. But like he knew I was thinking it, he stepped back. Out of range.

"I'm on your bumper. Let's go."

16
___

S^{am}

I KNEW EXACTLY what I was getting into at my parents' house. I knew this scene by heart. Dad somewhere on the spectrum of drunk between weeping and belligerent. Remorseful and absolutely bat-shit righteous. That was my father's spectrum. Mom would be in the living room, watching him through the curtains, forcing herself with all of her might not to bring him inside. She knew not to bring him in, because he only got meaner, drunker. Like a stray dog who kept pissing on the rug.

I pulled up in my truck, spraying snow as I skidded to a stop. Sophie had been on my bumper the whole way, blazing through every yellow light to stay with me. She knew where she was going, obviously, but she wanted to be with me when we got here.

She pulled to a stop behind me with less drama. I was

out of the truck before my father managed to get himself to his feet off the picnic table where he'd been sitting.

"Son?" he said, holding out his hand, stumbling sideways into the snow-covered bushes but catching himself. "Your mom's being unreasonable."

Belligerent on his way to righteous.

"Dad," I sighed. "You have to go."

"Go? This is my home!" Like clockwork he was going to launch into how he bought this trailer fifty years ago, but I needed him away from the door so that Sophie could go in and talk to Mom.

She stepped toward the door, like she was going to skirt around him, but he swiveled his big shaggy head her way. "Who are—hey, I know you."

"Hello Dale," she said. Calm and careful. "Merry Christmas."

"You still sniffing around this family?" Dad asked, turning to face me. "God, you got a whole..." he made this gesture like a dog panting at a table, begging for scraps "... thing with the Kanes."

"Dad, you need to leave."

"I bought this trailer!" he cried, stepping toward me, and Sophie darted around him and through the front door. I breathed a sigh of relief, imagining Sophie putting her strong arms around my mom's shoulders.

"Yeah, and you lost the right to walk in and out of it at will a bunch of years ago." I found myself in the ready position that was ingrained in my bones after so many years as a Marine.

I noticed how little he was wearing. His old camel-colored overcoat that used to make him look dashing was no protection against the cold. He was still lean, the wrinkles in

his face deeper. Thicker. Like he'd been thinking big, difficult thoughts. Which he hadn't.

His hair was gray and fell over his forehead in a thick
sweep.

When I was a kid , Mom had sent me into a bar to pull
him out because she couldn't stand to see him flirting with
other women, and I remembered women putting their
hands through that flop, running their fingers through it
while he told them the same old lies about losing his job at
the university, about how he'd worked in the labs with
people who were trying to cure cancer. He'd made it sound
like he'd been an integral part of operations, when he'd
been a temporary custodian who'd been fired for drinking
after three months on the job.

Mom once told me that the line he'd fed her was that he
was working at an advertising agency. Same reality, custodian—until he got caught stealing from the petty cash
drawer, but by then it had been too late. Mom was pregnant
with me.

"Dad," I said. "You gotta stop doing this."

"Visiting my wife. My home?"

"Pretending you care when you're only here because the
woman you've been lying to just came to her senses and
changed the locks on her door."

Dad sighed through his nose like a bull and fished his
flask out of his pocket.

Again— action before thought—I smacked the flask
right out of his hand and it went spinning into the bushes.

"Son. You're gonna go get that." The threat in his voice
used to work on me. Used to make me shake and tremble.
Mom, too.

"No. Listen, Dad, you're going to leave and you're not—"

He lunged for me. I mean, I couldn't believe the guy had

it in him. But I stepped sideways and he fell on his face in the snow. He tried to get up on his own but it was so disgraceful, so inept, I took pity on him and pulled him to his feet, holding him by the coat that let him get away with so much.

Hide from so much.

Pretend so much.

"You're going to stop this," I said. "You're going to leave Mom alone."

His face twisted into a sneer, but when he opened his mouth to say something, I simply applied pressure to his shoulder and elbow and he nearly collapsed at my feet. "This is done, Dad. You can't keep fighting something that's already happened."

"You going to beat up your old man?" he asked and I laughed.

"When I was sixteen, eighteen, that's all I wanted. It's why I joined the Marines, so I could beat the shit out of you. But I'm done with that. Done with you. So is Mom."

He made a sound like he knew she was in there thinking about the good years and fighting the urge to let him in.

"Tomorrow we're going to the police station and getting a restraining order. And, yeah, Dad, after that, if I see you here, I'll put you in the hospital just to give Mom a break from your shit."

He stood there for a second, a miserable man alone on a cold night.

"I never thought it would end like this," Dad whispered.

"How?"

He looked around, the tarnished exiled prince of a trailer park and a family who no longer wanted him. "Alone."

My father looked up at me, his eyes watery and...bleak.

And I wondered if there was any kind of difference between pushing people away by treating them like shit or treating yourself like shit.

Because that was what Dad and I were doing—pushing people away. Only our methods differed.

Dad wandered off, and part of me felt really, really bad for him. The way you would for any stray dog on a cold night. But inside that house was my mom, who didn't deserve any of this, and my job was being at her side.

I watched him go until the shadows ate him and his lying overcoat.

The inside of the trailer was warm and cozy. The tree blinked in the corner. The smell of coffee and cake in the air. It was the smell of home. And there on the couch was Mom, and beside her was Sophie, and that was the sight of home.

All my home. Right there. Right here.

Don't end up alone.

"Is he gone?" Mom asked, her eyes red from crying. I nodded.

"You all right?" I asked.

"Fine. Totally fine. I'm not even…it's just always such a shock when he shows up and it's always so…" She made a wild-eyed, crazy gesture.

"Dramatic," Sophie said.

"It's his addiction," I said. "That and the booze. He needs constant…churn."

"Well…" Mom sighed. "I need some peace and quiet."

"You want some more tea?" Sophie asked, and Mom picked up Sophie's hands and squeezed them.

"No, honey, you go on home. It's late."

Sophie kissed Mom's cheek and stood up, but then

paused. "What honey?" Mom asked, but Sophie smiled and shook her head.

"Nothing," she said. "Get some sleep. I'll come by tomorrow to see you."

Sophie walked past me and grabbed my hand. Everything about her felt like comfort. Looked like comfort. And I wished I could grab it with both hands. Hold her—with both hands. "Call me," she said, "if you need me."

I need you all the time.

"I will," I said and walked her out to her car, just in case my father was lingering. "What were you going to ask her?" My breath plumed in the cold night.

"Why she still loves him." She shrugged. "She does, you know. She still loves him. It's why she wants to let him in."

"I know," I said. "And he knows it. It's why he keeps coming around. Thanks for being here with me."

She kissed my cheek, her face pressed to mine. I breathed her in like air.

"If you want..." she said, and I knew what she was asking me.

"Yeah?"

"My door's open."

Was I strong enough to resist that? To say no to that?

I wasn't even sure why I was resisting anymore.

17

I watched her taillights vanish down the road toward downtown and went back inside to find my mother doing the dishes. Wiping the occasional tear with the wrist of her sweatshirt.

"Sit down, Mom. I can do that."

"Good, because I don't want to." She stepped away from the sink full of bubbles and sat down at the Formica kitchenette set where she always sat. For the crosswords. For an evening cigarette. For a morning cup of coffee.

"He won't come back tonight?" she asked, and I shook my head. "I'll go with you tomorrow to get that restraining order."

"Good," I said. She'd been putting me off for years.

"Sophie?"

"She went home," I said, putting a plate in the dish drainer. I felt the tips of my ears burn. The way my ears always burned these days when I talked about her. Thought about her. Tried not to think about her.

"Sam?"

"Yeah."

"Put down the sponge and look at me."

I turned and found her, my beautiful mother who should have had a million kids and a house by some water with a big tree in the back for her to sit under.

And she had me, this trailer, and my dad—the stray dog.

"I love you, Sam. I am so proud of you. There isn't a mother on this planet more proud of you."

"Am I getting buttered up for something?" I looked at her through one narrowed eye.

"Let that girl go. All the way. Or love her the way she deserves. Otherwise...you're damning her to half a life."

"Half a life?" I said like I didn't understand. But I did. This was my mother sitting here looking back with regret at the choices she'd made.

"I loved your father knowing he'd never love me the same way. The way I deserved. But he was so weak and I was even weaker—"

"Mom. Nothing about you is weak."

"That girl loves you, and she'll take anything you give her just so she can stay there. And if you let that happen, you're cruel. Your father is a weak man and he doesn't understand that. But you do."

A few days ago, before the party, I would have pretended not to understand. I would have told her our relationship wasn't like that. But the party had happened. This week had happened. And I'd tried to push her away with both hands. But Sophie...Sophie drove out here to sit by my mother's side. To help. And she'd do that every day if I wanted. And oh my God, did I want that.

"I love her,' I whispered.

"I know."

"I mean. Like...love her."

Mom laughed and then stood up and put her hand on

my face. "I know. And she loves you. It's all right to let it happen."

"How?" I asked, because that seemed to be the hard part.

"Stop fighting," she said. "Just stop fighting."

Sophie

I WAS NOT WAITING UP. I mean. It was after midnight but I was...you know, cleaning my crisper. Which is a thing a person should do every once in a while. Just as a rule. But even with the crisper clean and my floors swept and my laundry folded and actually put away, I couldn't pretend anymore.

He wasn't coming.

And, I mean, I couldn't blame him. His mom had been traumatized and his father was out there like some kind of ghost. A booty call had to be about the last thing on his mind.

So I brushed my teeth, washed my face. Turned off my light. And then, like I'd conjured him, there was a knock on the door.

While I had a whole history of playing it cool around him, my heart still skipped a beat.

I opened the door and there he was. Black hat. Frown. Hands braced on the sides of the doorway like he was holding himself back.

"Sam—"

"You shouldn't just...open the door. It's past midnight."

"I knew it was you."

"How?"

"Because I always know when it's you."

He came through that door like a freight train, kicking shut the door with his foot. Pulling me into my arms like he'd been lost without me.

His kiss was overwhelming. Everything I'd ever wanted. But I'd been here before and if I wasn't smart I'd be here again, exactly like this. Not knowing what he was thinking. Not knowing how he felt. And tonight I'd spent twenty minutes next to a woman who loved a man who didn't have enough respect or love for her to let her go.

I loved Sam's mom, but I couldn't live like that. I couldn't.

"Stop," I breathed against his mouth.

"Okay," he breathed against mine.

"You ignored me."

"I pretended to ignore you. Trust me...I can't ignore you. I can't look away from you."

"Are you being sweet because you want to get fucked—"

He kissed me again. Harder this time. He kissed me until I couldn't think. Until I was putty.

"Keep them off," he said as I reached for the lights. It was the two of us. And the dark. And what he'd said to my mom, and how I'd put my arm around his mom and let her cry into my neck.

But there was also the last week of his ignoring me and telling me to date Joe. And I wasn't going to go back in time. I wasn't going to just be grateful for his touch on my body. For his attention. For his kiss. Yeah, my gratitude had made me stupid. And I wasn't stupid.

"No," I said.

I turned on the lights and we blinked at each other like owls.

"I'm not doing this with the lights out. And I'm not doing it without looking at each other. If you're pretending I'm someone else—"

He stepped forward, hands around my face, his fingers caught in my hair, making my scalp sting. "Never." He swallowed and then again. "The last few years any girl I touched, any girl who touched me, whose hand *accidentally* touched mine when she handed me a drink and I thought...I *wished* it was you."

All those locks I'd put on my heart after the last time he split me open started to ease.

"You want the lights on?" he asked.

I nodded.

He dropped his hands from around my face and pulled off his hat. Unzipped his coat. Pulled his shirt over his head. And I realized what he was doing.

Lights on. Face to face. Naked.

He'd kept his shirt on last time, but this time...*oh my God.*

His chest...his shoulders. The bare, tender skin under his arms. The muscles of his stomach. Covered in so many scars. So many. Countless. I tried not to make a sound or react, but how was I supposed to do that?

"They're nothing," he said, running a hand over his chest like he was embarrassed. "Shrapnel. Rock. The rocks slice through everything. They're sharp."

"From the bullets?" I asked. "The bullets hit the rock and the rock...hits you?"

"Sometimes. Yeah. Half the time you don't even feel it," he said, like that made it better.

"This one is new?" I touched one at his collarbone.

"From the last deployment. The bullet hit my spotter, grazed my collarbone, and I fell back and cracked open my skull."

"Your helmet?"

"I'd...taken it off for a second. Stupid. My spotter was

being..." he swallowed "...well, I thought funny at the time, but it was just dangerous."

I had a million other questions but I knew when to push and when to ease off. It was time to ease off.

There was thick one near his armpit, at the edge, and I ran my thumb over it. To my surprise, to my utter delight, he twitched away, a smile ghosting over his lips.

I sucked in a breath. "You're ticklish."

"You try and you will be sorry."

"Gonna kill me with your bare hands?"

"No, but you'll be bent over that counter and it will be my hand against your bare ass."

"Is that supposed to deter me?" I lifted my hands my fingers, wiggling like I was going to go after him, and he dodged a little but grabbed both my hands in one of his and yanked me to him.

He smiled at me, and that top lock on my heart, the weakest of the three, just popped open.

"I didn't expect this."

"Yeah. I leave my shirt on a lot—"

"No. I didn't expect to laugh...like this...I mean. With you, like this."

He smiled, so sweet. "You're my best friend, Soph. Of course, this would be fun."

And he kissed me again. And then again. And his hands were under my sweater, cool against my skin and then warm. Then hot. He walked me away from the door toward the kitchen. We ran into a chair.

"Boots," I said. "You're wet."

"One of us is," he whispered, his hand cupping me through my jeans. I felt the the second lock tremble.

"Boots."

He laughed and we both ducked down, unlacing his

boots, yanking them off, in a hurry to get back to each other. He was so warm. So alive. Touching him, holding him felt like being plugged into a battery. His fingers made quick work of the button on my jeans and I shimmied them off, kissing his chest. He took off my bra, lifting me so he could get his mouth on me, and I wrapped my legs around his waist and let him carry me into the bedroom.

He turned on the bedside light, holding me with one hand, laying me down on the bed. I felt like I was made of light in his arms. And when he kissed my skin—where he kissed my skin the light broke through and we were bathed in it.

I opened the buttons on his jeans, pulling them off him, wanting to see what happened when I touched him. When I put my lips to his skin. If he was made of light, too. I made him stand, pushing his pants down so he could kick out of them. The underwear went with them and I held him in my hands. Kissed him. I didn't know if this beautiful, sexual, intimate thing was going to happen again. I didn't even feel like it was happening now. It was like some kind of dream.

But he was real in my hands. In my mouth.

"Fuck, Soph," he breathed, his fingers threading through my hair, pulling my hair out of the way so he could watch his dick fucking in and out of my mouth. "I...Soph."

Sam said nothing, as a rule. To say he was a man of few words was an understatement, so hearing him stammer the few he had was delicious. I squirmed on the edge of my bed.

"What do you need?" he asked, his voice a rough groan that made me squirm more. Made me ache.

"What do you need, Soph?"

I pulled back, his cock slipping out of my mouth, and I shot him an arch look. "I'm a little busy here."

"Oh my God," he breathed grinning down at me. "The mouth on you."

"Yeah. You love it."

"I do," he said, and his words went through me, and I wanted to stop and ask what he meant and did he mean *THAT*. But the second lock was already in danger, so I put the words aside and went back to sucking his dick.

He slipped his hand between my legs, shoving my thigh out wider so he could slip the whole of his palm up against me, but somehow that wasn't even enough. He pushed me away, onto my back, and fell down between my thighs.

"Sam—"

"I know what you need," he said.

And he did. Oh God, he did. His mouth and his fingers and I let him use all of it to push and pull me into an orgasm. I was sizzling light exploding all over the room.

"More," I said.

"Yeah." He laughed against me. Twisted his fingers inside of me to tease out another orgasm. But I needed more of him. More of his body against mine. More of his weight and his heat. I needed my legs around his waist and his lips against my mouth and his heart beating against mine.

"This," I said, pulling him up and over me. He put his hands beside my head and his hips pressed mine flat to the bed. "Inside, Sam. I need you inside."

"Yeah." Not just like he agreed, but he knew.

He got on his knees on the bed and shifted me forward, and then there was the slow, sweet press of him inside of me. And I gasped because it was a lot. He was a lot. He licked my throat, bit my chin, kissed my mouth.

He kissed me like I was home and he'd missed it so much.

That second lock blasted right open.

18

It took me a second after coming. To feel my feet. The top of my head. To be in my body again. But I felt him roll away. Shift away. Until there was space between us and all I could still feel was the heat of him.

"That was…" I said.

"Yeah."

"You've said that about a million times tonight."

"You make me speechless, Soph. What can I say?"

I smiled, turning my head to look at his profile, the scar right through his eyebrow. Tender and high on endorphins and the love leaking out of that second lock, I reached up to touch it. Run my finger along the raised edge of it.

He flinched, his hand coming up lightning fast to push mine away.

"Sam," I breathed, stunned.

"I'm sorry. I'm…" His eyes met mine, panicked and wide. He shook his head. "Sorry."

And then he was up and out of the bed and I was left there. Wondering why I was surprised.

"Hey!' I said, following him. Naked and well…naked. I

couldn't hide my love. My hurt feelings. My anger. "You said you wouldn't do this!"

"What am I doing?" he asked, pulling on his underwear and T-shirt and then handing me mine.

"What you said you wouldn't. Fucking me and leaving me like this. Ignoring me."

"I'm not leaving. I'm not ignoring. I just...wanted to be dressed to talk to you."

"To tell me why we can't do this again."

"No. Please... " And then I realized he was naked. Dressed, but naked. His face was still but ravaged. His eyes full of anxiety. He was just dressed; he wasn't leaving.

I pulled back all my anger and stood there.

"I want to talk to you. I do. Let me." He gestured back toward the bedroom, and I grabbed my sweater and put it on so I wouldn't feel quite so *naked* naked.

Back in my bedroom he crawled onto the bed and so I did too, and when he turned off the light I lay there in the dark beside him, like we had been seconds ago, but now we were awkwardly dressed. Awkwardly lying there. Just...awkward.

"I'm sorry," he said, his voice hushed in the dark.

"Any conversation in bed that starts like that isn't going to end well."

His laugh was a sharp, almost hard thing that made the bed shake a little. "The flinching...I have some lingering... stuff from the injury."

"The PTSD?" I asked. "Your mom told me."

I rolled over onto my side, facing him, tracing the arch of his nose and his forehead with my eyes.

"That's why you did the meditation room and the running thing?" he asked.

"I heard it helped." I shrugged, and to my surprise he

rolled over to face me, too, one arm under his head, the other stretched out along his body. I curled my knees up toward my chest and he lifted his knee to touch my toes and that third lock on my heart, the last lock, my very last lock, it shook.

"Heard that, did you?" he asked.

"I did some reading."

"Of course you did." He stroked my hair off my forehead with the flat of his hand. "And there's a lot of stuff that goes on with the PTSD. But I have brain damage from the concussion and they don't know when or if it will go away."

"What...what does the brain damage do?"

"It can...fuck up how I feel. Someone can touch me, and even if I know it should feel good, some wire gets crossed and it's like my skin is trying to crawl off my body."

I shifted away but he put his hand down on my knee. "And sometimes, with the PTSD and a shortened temper, I don't handle it well."

Every word was pulled from his lungs. I could hear it. Feel it.

"And I just thought you deserved to be with someone who felt what they were supposed to feel when you touched them."

"I think I know what I deserve."

"Someone who could take off their shirt and not feel like a freak," he said, not listening.

"Those are your words. Not mine."

"Who could be...easy with you."

"I happen to like difficult," I said.

"I don't want to be difficult."

"Stop. You're not...difficult. You're not. You're not damaged-"

"Sophie." He said my name like a scold.

"Not to me. Not to Wes. Your mom. The people at the company. To us you're not damaged." I expected him to argue but he only took a deep breath that shuddered and I realized how heavy that thought have been weighing on him. How badly he needed someone to come along and contradict it. "You're the most thoughtful person I know, Sam. You always have been. I don't know anyone who looks after people like you do. People you love. And who love you, but also total strangers. You've sacrificed so much to do it for people you'll never even meet. I think maybe... you can let us take care of you a little bit. Help you, when you need it."

"You do help me," he said.

"I'm not talking about blow jobs."

"I'm not either," he said. "You think I don't know everything you do for me?"

Of course he knew. He was the kind of guy who noticed everything. "How long have you known about my feelings for you?"

His smile was sweet and fleeting. "A while."

"That's why you pushed me away at the party."

"You looked beautiful at that party. I've never regretted saying something more than I regret not telling you that."

"Do you trust me?" I asked. Because really this was what it came down to in the end. We could go on and on about friendship and loyalty and helping each other when we needed it but if he wasn't ever going to trust me, we were done. Right now. "Really trust me. Not just to be good to you. But to know my own limits and boundaries and be good to myself."

"Yeah. I trust you."

"Then you trust me to know what I deserve."

He laughed. "I see what you did there. You're so clever, Soph."

"I am," I said with a smile. "Do you love me?"

"So much."

I poked him in the chest. "That's what I deserve. Someone who loves me. It's what you deserve too."

He was silent and I could feel how he still wanted to argue with me. The war was still happening in his head. His heart. "Does it happen all the time?" I asked. "Feeling the wrong thing when people touch you."

He shook his head.

"Can I touch you now?" I whispered, and he sighed.

"That's another thing I didn't want for you," he said. "Asking permission to touch the guy you're with. It's ridiculous."

"I don't know, consent is sexy." He laughed a little when I said it, which was the point. "Can I?"

"Yeah."

I stroked his hair back from his forehead, watching his face for a flinch. Watching to see if he was hiding it. "I'm not scared of you," I whispered. "Are you scared of me?"

"So much. I can't..." He shook his head.

"I've never had someone fight for me the way you do. The way you always have. I've never had..." He shook his head. "Meditation room? I mean, who does that? For me?"

"Half those guys just take a nap in there."

"I don't care what they do in there," he said. "You made that place for me. And I go in there every day and marvel. I just fucking marvel that you are in my life."

"Say it again," I said.

"I marvel—"

"That you love me."

He kissed my nose. My lips. "I love you," he said. "I love you so much I literally don't know what to do with myself.

Like, Sophie, I'm a mess. I can't be with you. I can't be without you. I need you to take pity on me."

"Never," I said. "I've never pitied you."

His beautiful eyes met mine and I saw right down deep into the heart of him. Where the holes his father tore out of him were scabbed over. Where the new holes from his injury were still bleeding.

"I love you so much I made our lunch room into a meditation room. I love you so much I wore a thong. And did you see those shoes?"

"I did."

I cupped his face in my hands. "I love you," I whispered. "I always have. I always will. Do you trust that?"

"Yeah," he said and I could tell he wanted to argue. To warn me about the dangers of loving him. But I knew those dangers and I loved him despite of them. Because of them.

Funny how a few days ago, I was sure the future of us needed me to be dressed up like someone I wasn't. And really, what Fucking Sam Porter and I needed was to be as naked as we could be.

And I planned on staying that way for as long as possible.

19

———

S am

I CAME AWAKE like I always did. In a heartbeat. Cataloging risks and realities. But I realized I was safe. Warm. Sophie a soft, snoring heap on the bed beside me. *Sophie.*

We should get a dog, I thought. *That's what this bed needs. A dog.*

Or a baby.

I looked at the wild mess of Sophie's hair peeking up from the edge of the covers. A girl with her hair. Her guts. My...well, I could teach her to throw a baseball or something. Make her eggs in the morning. Put in ponytails.

Carefully, I eased out of the bed, making sure not to wake her up. She rolled and sighed and started to snore again, and I felt like my whole body might just explode with happiness. The floors were cold and I hopped to the kitchen to fire up her coffee maker and see what she had that could be made into breakfast. The inside of her fridge was predictable. Eggs, ketchup, four jars of pickles. I grabbed the eggs and opened the freezer where she kept her bread.

A silver coil of Christmas ribbon fell down over the ice tray from the top of the fridge.

My gift was up there. Unopened.

"What are you doing?" Sophie asked, stepping into the kitchen wearing her pretty blue robe and that pair of knee-high red socks.

"I was going to make us some breakfast."

"Coffee?"

I pointed at the pot.

"You didn't open this?" I put the present on the counter.

Her eyes opened wide and she all but sparkled. "I...forgot."

"Why didn't you open it when I brought it?"

"Because I was mad at you. I'm not anymore, so gimme." She sat down on the stool at her kitchen counter and pulled the present to her with both hands.

She pulled the ribbon and tore open the paper, and I vowed right at that moment to shower her with gifts. Nonstop. Just so I could watch the joy on her face. I was going to bring Christmas back to this woman, the way it should be. It was going to be Christmas albums and wreaths and real trees and eggnog. It would be the whole show, because Sophie deserved the whole show and I had an endless need to give it to her.

From the tissue paper she pulled out the silver combs I'd bought in the market a thousand miles and a lifetime ago.

"Sam," she breathed, looking up at me with tear-filled eyes.

"I saw them and thought of you."

"My hair?" she laughed.

"Actually," I whispered. "I thought of this."

I stepped behind her. I took in the sleep smell of her. The wild curls in my hands. The strong, beautiful set of her shoulders. Remembering what the teenage girl in the market had told me, I gathered her hair in my hands. Now I just needed to...*twist?*...the hair and put the combs in what felt like backwards and then...

Slowly, I stepped back, like any sudden moves and her hair would slip out of the combs. It didn't.

"There," I said. "I think that's how it works."

She stood up from the stool and went into the bathroom. I followed, really surprised that the combs were staying in place. Sophie stood in front of the mirror, turning to see how they held.

"How...how do they look?"

"Perfect," I said, not really talking about the combs. "I got them in a market."

"Where?"

"I...can't actually tell you."

She looked at me with wide eyes and I shrugged. "But I bought them and I imagined how they could give me an excuse to stand close to you and touch your hair and breath you in, because when I bought them I could not imagine a situation where you'd let me do that—without a reason."

"I've got lots of reasons," she said and came to put her arms around my waist where I stood in the door of the bathroom. "They're beautiful and I love them."

"So?" I asked, kissing her nose.

"So what?"

"I know you got me something."

"Oh, sweetheart—"

"Sweetheart? That's what we're going with? Sweetheart?"

"You want me to give you a different pet name?"

"I always imagined being called babe."

"This conversation is not happening."

"Then give me my present," I said, shaking her by her lean waist.

"Okay, but it's awful. It's like...a joke compared to these beautiful things," she said, squeezing past me and touching the combs.

In her bedroom she pulled out a red-wrapped gift and handed it to me. "I'm serious. It's terrible."

Inside was a new video game headset.

"I know you left your last one behind." She shrugged. "I told you it was lame."

I put down the controller and wrapped my arms around her, collapsing us onto the bed. "You know what I like best about it?"

"That it's wireless?"

"That I'm not going to need it," I told her. "I'm never playing another game with you from the other side of the world. I'm never going to have to message you. Or wait for you to wake up. Every game now, I'm on that beanbag, right next to yours. You can trash talk me to my face."

"You talking about moving in?" she asked, and I paused.

"I wasn't trying to jump ahead—"

"Let's go get your stuff," she said.

"In a minute," I said, kissing my way down to those red socks I loved so much.

20

———

S ophie

"YOU DO NOT NEED to be nervous," I told him as we stood on the sidewalk in front of Wes's townhouse. Wes and Penny's townhouse.

"I'm not."

There was a wreath on the door. That was new. I sniffed it. Real pine with a pretty red bow. Penny's touch. My brother wouldn't know a wreath from a wrecking ball.

"Can we go in?" Sam asked.

"Sure." But I didn't step forward and Sam, sweet Sam, just stood beside me in the cold.

"You don't need to be nervous either," he told me.

"Wes said he invited your mom *and* my mom. How can you not be nervous?"

"It's a party. Lots of people go to parties."

"We hate parties," I grumbled. This party was just

supposed to be small. Steak and booze and people I loved. "What if my mom says something mean to your mom?"

"She won't."

"Have you met my mom?"

He laughed, but it didn't make me feel better.

Behind us an Uber pulled up, opened, and W.B. got out of the back seat and ran around the car to open the door for Joy to hop out. Joy said something that made him laugh, and then she leaned forward and kissed W.B. square on the mouth.

"Ah-ha!" I shouted. "I knew it."

"Knew what?" Sam asked.

"Them. You!" I turned as Joy and W.B. came to stand with us. "I knew you had a thing for him."

"I suppose did." Joy smiled. "Maybe a little."

"Is there something wrong with the door?" W.B. asked. "Or are we standing in line?"

"And Sam?" Joy asked me in a low voice. " You never did tell me what happened at the holiday party."

"The...ah...makeover worked," I said.

"The makeover was bullshit," she said. "It was all you being you."

I leaned back, holding her by the shoulders. "Happy New Year," I said to her, this fun new friend.

She laughed. "We're off to a pretty great start."

"Can we go in?" W.B. asked. "Or is there a problem with the door?"

"Come on," Sam said, taking the bull by the horns and pushing open the front door. "Hey!" he cried as Wes stuck his head around it.

"Penny!" Wes yelled over his shoulder. "They're done standing around outside."

Penny stepped into the foyer, pushing her glasses up

higher on her nose and smiling... no, beaming at all of them. "Hi! Happy New Year!"

There was the kicking off of snow and hanging up of coats. Penny shuffled us into the kitchen. It was a sleek modern kitchen that had cupboards with no handles and stainless steel appliances. I always thought it looked cold but with Wes standing there smiling so hard, I realized that the cabinets were actually a warm brown and the lighting was nice and soft and anyplace looked better when the people inside of it were in love.

Penny took down champagne glasses that I'd never seen before in Wes's house while my brother popped a bottle of the good stuff. "Is Mom here?" I asked him as he poured and I handed full glasses to W.B. and Joy.

"Not yet."

"She's coming?"

He shrugged.

"Is this a joke?" I asked.

"It's a party," he said. "Try and relax." He poured the last of the champagne into my glass and then tossed his arm around my shoulder. "I'd like to make a toast," he said and we all lifted our glasses.

But then my brother, who was never at a loss for words looked over at Penny and was silent.

And then, to my surprise, it looked like my brother got tears in his eyes. *Oh Lord, this is gonna be a weird night.*

"To love," he finally said and Penny beamed.

"And surprises," Joy added.

"And friendship," Sam said and tears were suddenly hot in my eyes. We all clinked glasses.

"Come on, dig in!" Penny said and pulled out little plates – something else I'd never seen and we all dug into the big, gorgeous cheese tray on the island. Wes refilled our glasses and got Sam a beer and then...within minutes it was a party. It was all my friends. All this love. Sam was laughing at something Wes said, and Penny was telling us the story of how Wes *actually* proposed, for real—in, of all places, a divorce lawyer's office. And I felt myself losing my worry about the one thing that might ruin all this fun - my mom.

There was a knock and I didn't bother to brace myself, but when Sam's mother came through the door I was relieved and I couldn't pretend I wasn't.

"Happy New Year," Betty said and Sam, Wes, and I rushed to hug her and take her coat and Penny took the cake she'd baked.

"It's not that gingerbread," Betty assured me. "Just chocolate."

"It's perfect," I said.

"Champagne?" Wes asked Betty, and she shrugged with a coy smile. She wore a fancy sweatshirt that said PARTY in rainbow sequins.

"One won't hurt."

And then it was Sam and Betty and me standing in the hallway. "So?" She blinked at us from behind her glasses. "You two have something to tell me? A late Christmas present, maybe?"

"Mom," Sam said, rebuked.

"I love him so much," I blurted, and Betty's eyebrows lifted. "I have for so long."

"I know," she said, squeezing my shoulder.

"I love her, too. For just as long," Sam said.

"I know," Betty said with a nod. "I'm just glad you two have finally figured it out. Have you talked? Really talked?"

"Yes," Sam said. "I told her about the PTSD and the concussion and—"

"He agreed to therapy."

Betty's eyebrows went sky high and she let out a sigh so deep it was like she was deflating.

"I'm so glad. I'm so..." She kissed my cheek hard and then kissed her son's cheek hard. "Damn happy. It's the best Christmas present a mother could get."

I felt that doubt I didn't want to feel about how my own mother would not respond to this news with the same joy. And I hated it. I hated that it bothered me. That it might in any way hurt Sam.

"Come on," Sam said, putting his arms around both of us. "There's a cheese tray in here you should meet."

Back in the kitchen another bottle of champagne was opened and I drank a glass. Maybe too fast—that was debatable.

Joy was explaining the success of her porn ornament line, something W.B. was clearly horrified by, and soon there was another bottle of champagne and even Sam was laughing. Like really laughing. Like bracing himself on my shoulder and laughing, and I hadn't seen him that easy in so long that it went to my head with the champagne.

"Mom!" Wes cried, and we all turned to see my mother standing in the doorway to the kitchen, wearing a pair of jeans and a frown.

And just like that all the laughter dried up to coughs.

"I don't mean to interrupt," she said with a careful smile that did two things to me at the exact same time. Made me feel bad for her and made me tense every single muscle in my body like I was expecting to be punched.

"You're not." Penny stepping into the breach was the bravest thing I'd ever seen. "Can I take your coat?"

Mom hesitated, like she wasn't sure if she was going to stay, but then handed Penny the coat. Joy tried to continue the story about the porn ornaments but the damage had been done. A thick black cloud was all over everything, my mother's doing.

"Champagne?" Wes asked Mom, and she opened her mouth in that tight way that usually indicated she was about to say something awful. Something mean. But then, to my total shock, she took a breath and smiled.

"I think I should go," Mom said. "I think, no matter what I do, I don't do it right."

She turned for the door, and in the silence she left behind Sam and I looked at each other, and I saw his support no matter which way I went with this. And it gave me the strength to take the high road, after so many years of taking no road when it came to my mother.

"Mom!" I said and chased after her, finding her at the door with Penny handing her her coat.

"Please stay," Penny was saying, because she, too, was a good egg. "It's a holiday and we haven't had much of a chance to know each other."

"Maybe we can have lunch," Mom said, brittle and cool.

"Mom. Stay." I stepped up, feeling Sam at my back. "I haven't seen you—"

"Whose fault is that?" she snapped and then sighed. "I haven't gone anywhere. I haven't done anything. I've been here...waiting."

"Mom," I breathed and stepped forward. "Let's change it. Right now. Let's...change everything. We don't have to be like this."

Mom's eyes went over my shoulder to Sam.

"He's in my life, Mom," I said.

"I know. And...I'm glad. And..." Her smile looked a little bit like it might break her face. Like her muscles didn't work that way. "Sorry. For everything."

"Forgiven," Sam said, like it was easy. Like it was all just that easy. I reached back for his hand and he grabbed it. We could do that too. Mom and me.

"Mom," I said. "If you leave, nothing is going to change. I know it. You know it. But if you stay..."

"Why is it on me?" she asked through a tiny pinched mouth.

"Because it is. And you know it. You've been mean my whole life and I'm done trying to make it right. You try, mom. Just stay and have a drink. And try."

Mom glanced up into the corner of the hallway with such attention I actually turned to see if there was a spider or something up there. There wasn't. Mom was just being ...Mom.

I sighed and started to turn, not ready to give my mother any more of my holiday. Or my happiness.

"I was so scared of you being hurt that I ended up hurting you first," Mom blurted and I turned back around, slowly. "I know that doesn't make sense."

"Well, no one is going to be asking you to write a parenting book," I joked, but Mom's face crumpled.

"I was just so unhappy and I should have been better to you kids, I know that. And I'm sorry. I'm so sorry."

"Mom. Mom." I took one step forward, and then another, and then I was hugging my mom. And she was hugging me back and I had only waited twenty-five years for this to happen with no idea how badly I needed it. My mom. Hugging me.

"Sam is a good man," Mom said.

"I'm glad you noticed."

"He won't hurt you like your father hurt me. Hurt us."

"No. He won't. But you should get to know him better."

Mom leaned back. "I should get to know you better, too, I think."

"And Wes and Penny," I said, because I was a loyal sister.

Mom nodded and stepped away from me towards the kitchen, where without my mother's wet blanketness, Joy was finishing her story and everyone was laughing.

I didn't follow her in and because Sam was with me whereever I might go, he lingered with me in the hallway.

"You coming in?" Mom asked us.

"Just a second," I said.

"Look at you," Sam said when it was just the two of us and the coat closet. "Getting along with your mom."

"A real Christmas Miracle."

He wrapped me in his arms. "I'm proud of you."

"I'm a little proud of me too," I said and kissed his chin and then his lips. And his lips one more time.

"You know," he said. "I had this thought-"

"Is it about having sex in the coat closet because I had that thought too."

"No," he laughed. "But, maybe? The thought was that I had stolen Christmas from you."

I leaned back. "How?"

"Because you weren't meant to be mine. None of this... was meant to be mine. And I took it from you, one kiss at a time."

"See," I said, walking backwards towards the coat closet and pulling him with me. "That's where you're wrong. You were always meant to be mine. Always."

"We can't have sex in that coat closet," he said when I opened the door.

He was right, but still. "Then you owe me."

"What exactly do I owe you?" He narrowed his eyes and I leaned up on tip toe to whisper the dirtiest things I could think of. "Well," he coughed, his neck and cheeks all flushed. "We could leave. Now. I could do half of that in the car."

There was a pop of another bottle of champagne and more laughter. Betty. My mom. All our family and friends.

"Later," I said. And we went into the kitchen where the awkward little party was getting slightly less awkward. His hand slipped from my shoulder to my waist and then he was holding my hand. And I was holding his so tight I was never going to let go.

He gave me love and joy and happiness. He gave me sweaty orgasms and filthy sex. He gave me a new way to look at my past and a future so bright I could hardly stand it.

I was the luckiest girl on the planet because every day with Fucking Sam Porter was Christmas.

THANK you thank you thank you for picking up HOW MY BROTHER'S BEST FRIEND STOLE CHRISTMAS! If you haven't read the other books in the series - one click now!

My Fake Christmas Fiancé

Santa Baby Maybe

If you want more sexy family drama - don't worry! I've got you covered. Turn the page for an excerpt of THE TYCOON

The cruel and beautiful man who ruined my life has everything he wants—everything except me.

FIVE YEARS AGO, Clayton Rorick loved me. Or so I thought. Turned out he only wanted to get his hands on my daddy's company. Heartbroken, I ran away with nothing but the clothes on my back. Like a twisted Cinderella. When my father dies, leaving my sisters in a desperate situation, it's up to me to help them.

I'LL HAVE to beg the man who broke my heart to save us.

BUT CLAYTON HASN'T FORGOTTEN me and what he wants in exchange for his help is...my body, my heart and my soul.

Prologue
VERONICA

NO ONE HAD EVER TOLD me about orgasms.

Like, I had a sense, from movies or whatever. But no one ever gave me the complete picture. How they were tricky. How you had to be patient and vulnerable. Naked in a lot of ways—more than just, you know, actually naked. No one told me that they were a little frightening, that feeling of chugging up the incline of a roller coaster. Of something powerful and scary being just over the edge of a cliff.

Really, what no one told me was how freaking consuming they were.

After having some (eight, to be exact), it was literally all I could think about. Even in this stupid dress with the suffocating shapewear and the itchy netting. The boning in the bodice that dug into my armpits and didn't let me breathe. The way my boobs—always a problem, except in the orgasm department—were squished and flattened.

All of this should be awful. But it wasn't. Not really.

Because it was my engagement party.

And all I could think about was sex.

And Clayton.

"You didn't lose the ten pounds you were supposed to, did you?" my stepmother, Jennifer, asked. She had her disapproving sniff going at full speed.

"Nope," I answered.

"Veronica," she said and then sighed, the most disappointed sigh. "You were going to try."

"Was I?"

Clearly, while I'd been thinking about sex, my stepmother had been thinking about the ten pounds she wanted me to lose. The urge to tell her to just calm down, was hard to resist, but I managed -- because orgasms. I used to obsess over those ten pounds, too, and all it got me was another five.

But this was what she'd done to my half-sister, Sabrina. She'd tried to bully and shame her into a size zero. The woman just couldn't stand to see a girl eat bread. Or be happy.

I would never understand how my father could go from my beautiful, loving mother to Jennifer. They were diametrically opposed.

"Tonight..." Jennifer said, straightening herself up so she looked like the stick that had been stuck up her ass. She wore a blue dress that hugged her body so closely I could practically see her hip bones through the material. "...is important."

I was twenty-two, not twelve. And it was my freaking night and no one needed to tell me what was important. I turned to face her instead of dodging her gaze in the mirror and I looked right at her. Something I never would have had the courage to do before the last few weeks with Clayton.

But I've had eight mind-bending orgasms—and they'd

brought me some kind of new confidence I'd never had before.

"Jennifer," I said, right in her frowny face. "It's my engagement. It's my party. It's my body. And none of it concerns you."

Jennifer sniffed so hard she nearly turned herself inside out.

Behind me, Trudy swallowed a laugh. She'd been brought into the upstairs dressing room of The King's Land Ranch to literally sew me into my dress—no zippers for the girl who didn't lose the ten pounds.

"We're nearly done," Trudy said around the mouth full of pins between her lips. A few more tugs and twitches on my dress and she stood back and smiled at me. *"Eres bonita."*

I believed my old friend when she said I was pretty, because for one of the few times in my life—I felt pretty. I felt it down in my bones. Tonight was going to be amazing.

"Gracias."

Trudy helped me down from the dais where I'd been standing surrounded by mirrors. A thousand reflections of myself stared back at me. It wasn't pleasant.

"Do you know where my sister is?"

"Where do you think your sister is?" Trudy asked with a laugh, sticking the pins she'd had in her mouth into the pincushion she wore on her wrist.

I sighed. The stables. Probably in her dress, too.

"What have I said about speaking in Spanish, Veronica?" Jennifer asked.

"More than half the people who live on this ranch speak Spanish," I said, shaking out the skirt of my sparkly tea-length gown. "You could try learning it. But if you don't want to hear it, you should move."

Jennifer stepped up to me so fast she was like a snake

coming out of the bushes. And her face...uh-oh...I'd pissed her off.

I tried not to smile.

"I have spent the last sixteen years thinking this day would never come. That you would never find a man to get you out of this house. But it's here and I'm so glad you are leaving." She spat her venom all over the place. And once upon a time her words would have hurt, more than hurt, maybe. But Clayton and the orgasms were like armor. "You and your alcoholic sister need to just get out of my house."

"Bea's not an alcoholic," I said, but Jennifer was already leaving. "She's just fun!" I shouted at her back.

And then it was just me and Trudy in this stupid hall of mirrors.

Trudy touched my back, trying to be comforting, but if I had armor around myself, my weak spot was Beatrice. I would have left this house a long time ago if it hadn't meant leaving Beatrice here. Sabrina, too, for that matter.

Someone had to take care of them.

"Don't let her get to you. Tonight is too special," Trudy said.

Right. I was twenty-two. Sabrina a year out of high school. I could have this life. The orgasms and Clayton.

The whole fairy tale.

"You deserve to be happy." Trudy eyed me sideways, a smile on her face. She was married to Oscar, who ran my father's stables, and while not employed officially by the King family, she'd stepped in when my mom died and has always been really good to me and Bea. A motherly buffer between us and our stepmother.

We hugged and Trudy left to change her clothes. Her hair was already done, with the white mock-orange flowers from the shrubs behind the house tucked into her curls. I had the same in mine. Well, sort of. They were already slipping out. I turned in the mirror so I could try and tuck them back in, but it wasn't much help. My brown hair was so straight it was impossible to get things to stay. I was doing my best with the bobby pins, but I didn't have my glasses and my fingers looked like pink blurs in a bigger brown blur.

"Hello, Veronica."

Oh, God. A tide of heat rolled over my body and the bobby pin dropped from my suddenly numb fingers.

It was Clayton. And, just like that, I was breathless. Hot.

He stood in the doorway, a black blur that became clear as he walked toward me. My God, that man in a tux. It shouldn't be legal. He was handsome enough without the bespoke black coat and crisp white shirt, but with them he was nearly unbearable. His dark hair was swept back from his face. And I didn't know if you could call a face dangerous, but if you could, his was. His nose was maybe too big, his cheekbones too sharp. His resting face was utterly unreadable with perhaps a hint of disdain. His eyes were a penetrating dark brown. Nearly the color of his hair. But his lips. His lips were the rudest thing I'd ever seen. Thick and full. Slow, painfully slow, to smile.

And they tasted so good.

He looked like one of those intense Irish actors. Broody and dark. And the way he watched me; it was like he couldn't wait to take me apart with his teeth and put me back together with poetry.

He was the brightest thing I'd ever seen and I had to look away. Look away or go blind. Or go crazy. Or strip this damn dress off and ask him to do what he did to me in his office last week.

"Let me help you."

"With what?"

"The flower?" He crossed the dressing room and crouched at my feet. I stared up at the ceiling and prayed for strength. For calm.

Just...be cool, Ronnie.

He stood holding the mock-orange blossom in his fingers. The smell, thanks to my crushing of the delicate thing, filled the small space between us. It was heady. Like champagne on an empty stomach.

"Where does it go?" he asked.

"My hair...but I can't—"

"You're not wearing your glasses."

I used to think he never smiled. When I met him four years ago, he was humorless. Stern. None of the Irish poet, only the businessman Dad had hired to manage the amalgamation of some of his companies.

But in the last six months, as we started dating he smiled more.

And I knew that was because of me.

He brought me orgasms. I brought him smiles.

Not sure if it was fair, but it was real.

"Why aren't you wearing your glasses, Veronica?"

"They don't go with the dress."

He put his hands to my waist and I swallowed a moan low in my throat.

Kiss me, I thought. *Please, just kiss me. Let's not go downstairs. Let's not do this whole party. Let's shut the door and take off these clothes...*

He turned me until I faced the mirror and it was everything I could do not to close my eyes. I hadn't looked in the mirror while Trudy was sewing me into my dress, or earlier, when Sabrina was helping me with my makeup.

I didn't know myself in this moment, so instead I looked at Clayton.

I couldn't say I knew him any better, but he was so damn fun to look at.

"You're nervous?" he asked. His fingers found my bobby pin and tucked the flower back into the elaborate twist that was my hair.

"A little."

"Me, too."

I laughed. "I don't believe you."

"Why?" he asked. Our eyes met in the mirror and it was a strange, diffused connection. Painfully intimate.

"You don't seem nervous about anything. Ever."

Clayton projected a kind of detachment. An unruffled coolness. He was the picture of control. Except... I thought of that time in his office. And again in his condo. That last date when he'd cooked for me.

He hadn't been cool then. His hands had shaken when his fingers combed through my hair, when he held my skull in his palms. His voice had broken when he moaned, "So good, Veronica. You suck me so good."

Between my legs I suddenly throbbed.

"You're beautiful."

It was weird. Well, maybe not weird, but he always said I was beautiful. He never said I looked beautiful. Every compliment I'd ever gotten on my looks had been about the dress I was wearing or how I'd done my hair. The implication being that without adornment I was not beautiful.

But Clayton was not commenting on the fancy Oscar de le Renta gown. Or my hair. Or the smoky eyes Sabrina had given me.

He was talking about me. Myself. My body. The skin I lived in.

It wasn't something you noticed until someone said it to you repeatedly. Especially a man like him. Not just that he was handsome or that he was sexy.

It was that he was never wrong.

"This dress," he whispered, and his fingertips brushed over the strapless bodice. Not quite touching my breasts but close enough that I knew he was doing it on purpose. "Is perfect for you."

He hummed low in his throat. And his hand ran from my breast down my waist to my hip. The dress was seven thousand layers of pink tulle with gold sparkles and crystals sewn into every layer. The bodice was fitted but the skirt flared out at my waist. Not poufy, just...forgiving.

It was a beautiful dress and I felt beautiful in it. Except that it was too tight.

"I have something for you," he said.

"Clayton," I sighed. "You don't have to give me anything."

The ring on my finger, the orgasms. The happiness I felt. All of it was enough. Except...well, he could tell me he loved me. That would be something. A gift.

Two months ago, after we'd had sex for the first time (after the first two of my orgasms), we were lying in the big king-size bed in his home, sweating into his sheets, and I'd blurted that I loved him. He'd kissed me, given me the third orgasm. And the next day he proposed.

Maybe he didn't love me. Maybe he just liked me a lot. Maybe he was pretty sure that he would love me at some point, and just wasn't there yet.

Or maybe...just maybe...he did love me, and he just didn't know how to crack through that armor he had around him.

I voted that option. Because there was no reason for him to do the things he did unless he felt something real for me.

And because I didn't want it to be awkward, I hadn't told him I loved him again. Except a few times when he'd fallen asleep before me, the dark splash of his hair falling down on his forehead. Those rude-boy lips parted as he breathed.

At that moment I couldn't resist and the words slipped out in a whisper against the skin of his shoulder. Secrets I kept in the night.

Clayton pulled an oblong box out of the inside pocket of his tuxedo jacket and my stomach fluttered. He was so good at picking out jewelry for me. My engagement ring was an antique Tiffany-set sapphire. Elegant, with a bit of filigree around the impressive stone to make it unique. It was my favorite thing in the world.

He handed me the box with the half curl of his lips that made him seem so boyish. I wanted to hug him. Tousle his hair. Whisper *I love you* against the pulse in his neck.

"Open it," he said.

"You don't have to—"

"I know."

I opened the box and in it was a beautiful necklace. Antique. Victorian, maybe. A long gold chain with a diamond and pearl pendant. A giant diamond.

"I saw it and thought of you." He took it out of the box to put it around my neck where the chain and jewels glittered and gleamed in the lights and mirror. The touch of his fingers against my nape made my breath hitch.

"I have something for you, too," I said, and stepped away from his touch over to where I had put my clothes. My jeans and Converse. My purse. I pulled out the box for him.

This might be a mistake. So dumb. I mean, the man had no need for something as old-fashioned as this. But...I saw it and thought of him. I held the box out.

He seemed weirdly flabbergasted. Like he didn't know

what to do with the package I was offering him. Or maybe like he didn't want it. He looked at the box and then at me, his armor totally in place.

How, I wondered in the back of my brain, have I managed to get engaged to a man I can't read? Like, what kind of lunacy was that?

"You can open it later." Embarrassed, I started to put the box back in my purse, humiliation a copper taste in the back of my mouth.

"No," he said. "No, please, I'd like to open it now."

I handed it back to him and wiped my sweating hands on my gown. Which was shit for that kind of thing, actually. The netting stuck to my fingers.

Clayton pulled one end of the red ribbon that made the elaborate bow on top of the small box and it was like he was pulling my stomach with it. I reached into my purse and grabbed my glasses.

My own armor, maybe.

Or maybe I just wanted to see his face clearly when he opened my present.

He pulled off the thin lid and lifted the antique gold pocket watch out of the box.

"Veronica," he breathed.

"I saw it in a shop on Lucas Street. I mean, it's a little silly, I guess. But it does keep time. The guy at the store said it was owned by a cattle rancher in the area in the 1800's."

He turned the watch over and hit the small knob that popped open the front.

"That inscription was there," I said, wanting some distance from it if it was too much. Though the inscription was part of the reason I bought it. Because the woman who gave her husband this watch over a hundred years ago had had more courage than I did.

"For you, forever," he read.

"It's—"

He said nothing, just stepped toward me, stalked toward me, really, so fast and with such power I took a step back and my head hit one of the mirrors. And then he was kissing me. His hands cupped my face, like he was holding me still. Like I might possibly run?

Please.

These kisses, like he was trying to communicate something to me with his tongue, were a huge part of the reason I said yes when he asked me to marry him. Because this felt so important and real. His hands on my body. His tongue against mine.

It filled me with power, the kind of power that was bigger than I am.

It was epic.

He pulled back, rested his forehead against mine. "Thank you," he breathed. His breath smelled like mint and me.

"Thank you," I said back, and we smiled at each other. I beamed with all my heart, and his lip curled in a half grin, barely there.

"I might have messed up your hair," he said, pulling me away from the mirror. The flower he'd tried to put back fell to the floor.

"It's fine," I said. "Leave it. I don't think that flower was meant to be."

He clicked open the watch. "We need to head downstairs."

"Right." I smoothed my dress and reached to take off my glasses.

"Leave them," he said.

"Jennifer—"

"Hardly matters. Leave them. The whole point of tonight is for you to enjoy yourself. To have the kind of party that you deserve. I want you to enjoy tonight and you can't do that if you can't see." He touched my glasses, straightening them on my face.

"Well, when you put it that way." I twisted my lips. "Though I don't know how much of tonight will be enjoyable."

"Try," he said.

The idea of flaunting this relationship to Dallas's elite made me want to cringe. But I considered it my going-away gift to Dad and Jennifer. I'd do this dumb thing because they wanted it, and then I was done.

Because in one month's time my life as a King would be over and I'd be a Rorick.

Veronica Rorick.

With so many hard consonant sounds I was practically a fortress. I loved it.

He kissed me again. "See you down there."

After he walked out of the dressing room I folded forward, putting my hands on my knees.

Jesus. That man I was going to marry was so damn potent.

"Oh, my gosh! Ronnie!"

The whirling dervish that was my half sister rushed into the room. She was just a few months younger than my sister, Bea, because my father was a cheating asshole and barely waited until my mother was in the ground before making his mistress the next Mrs. King so he could continue his search for a son in the wombs of his wives.

I should hate Sabrina, by rights, but it was impossible to hate Sabrina.

Shallow as a puddle, but sweet as sugar.

"You are a dream!" She was all lit up from the inside because the girl loved a party and tonight's was going to be a good one. A blowout, as she called it. "You're gorgeous. That dress! Your hair! That necklace! Are you sure about the glasses?"

"Sabrina," I sighed.

"Of course, your call. Totally your call." She stood in front of me and beamed. She was lovely and I couldn't help but smile back at her. We both had my father's dark hair, but her eyes were dark, too. Sabrina used to be a roly-poly preteen but in the last few years she had sculpted herself into the kind of perfection that made Jennifer giddy.

But perfection was so hard.

"I saw your gorgeous guy leaving. Is that why your lipstick is a mess?"

"Is it?" I pulled open my purse for the lipstick Sabrina had loaned me.

"Let me. You can't draw a lip to save your life."

Sabrina plucked the lip liner and gloss from the inside of my bag and got right up into my personal space. That was kinda Sabrina's thing. No boundaries.

"Sooooo..." she said.

"Yeah."

"I heard Dylan was invited."

Our half brother.

"He won't come."

Sabrina projected so much hope. She'd followed him around like a puppy the summer he'd stayed with us. We all had. He still left and never came back. "Hank said—" Sabrina had refused to call our father by any other name.

"He won't come because of Dad, Sabrina. Trust me. If there's one thing you can count on with Dylan, it's that he wants no part of being a King."

She pouted and I did, too. Which must have been the right thing to do because she beamed at me as she finished the makeup repair.

"You look perfect."

"You know..." I said, like it was a surprise—which it was "...I feel kinda perfect."

She wrapped me in her thin arms and I hugged her back. "Garrett Pine is here," she whispered.

Oh, boy.

In addition to Dallas society, we'd invited the entirety of the town of Dusty Creek, the arid clutch of churches and bars with one school, a medical clinic, and a grocery store that was about five miles away from the ranch.

Bea, Sabrina, and I all went to high school there with varying degrees of success and happiness.

And Garret Pine was a big part of that town.

And Sabrina loved him like a lunatic.

"He brought his fiancée."

"Oh, honey," I breathed. "I'm so sorry."

"I'm not," she said. "I'm happy for him. Delighted." She smiled so bright it almost blinded me to the heartache she couldn't quite hide.

"Don't do anything crazy," I told her.

"I won't."

"Sabrina," I sighed. "I mean it. No more stunts."

She pulled a face. "I won't do anything except make him sorry he'll never be mine by being charming and amazing."

"Well, you do look amazing."

"So, do you, Ronnie," she said. "Emma Stone's publicist is here, too. And some TV executives. I'm going to go show them my star power."

I hoped that didn't mean her underwear.

And then she was gone, leaving the smell of her perfume and a sense of glitter in the air behind her.

I trusted Sabrina's reaction to my reflection more than my own judgment, so I didn't bother looking back into the mirror. Outside the dressing-room door, I turned left instead of right and headed down the back staircase.

"Veronica!" called a voice behind me and I turned, wishing I'd moved just a little faster.

James Court.

Ugh.

"Hello, James," I said with a reserved smile. Which didn't seem to matter. I could be cold and reserved and downright rude, and it never seemed to matter to this guy.

James worked at King Industries and was one of my father's favorites.

"The boy's got swagger," Dad always said.

Which meant he had an ego and sense of entitlement a mile wide.

I hated him and I had no idea why, in the last six months, he'd gotten so interested in me.

"Congratulations," he said, tipping his glass of scotch toward me—a little too much and some of the scotch slipped out. "The best man won. I should have seen that coming, I suppose."

He was drunk.

I took a step back, keeping my smile small. "If you're referring to Clayton, you're right."

He took another step forward, so close I could smell his hot breath. His blue eyes narrowed. *Mean*, I thought. *This guy is just mean.*

"You're going to figure out sooner or later your old man made a mistake picking that fucker."

"Jimmy, you're drunk," I said and put my hand up to

push him away. I took four quick backward steps before I turned.

"You're not even the hot sister," he yelled after me. Like that was a newsflash.

Around the edge of the hallway I stopped to get my breath and calm myself down. So many assholes were trying to ruin my night.

I needed my sister and a drink.

And some cheese.

The kitchen was full of black-vested and white-gloved staff, and I ducked out the back door, grabbing a skewer of grilled halloumi and figs as a server walked by.

Delicious.

Another thing they didn't tell you about orgasms. They made everything better.

Even cheese, which I honestly didn't think could *be* better.

The moon was swollen and low in the endless indigo sky and the air smelled like the grills behind the long screened-in porch—hickory smoke and twilight. The stables in the distance looked like a mansion, with turrets and bright, sparkling windows. All the horses, the stable cats, and Sally the collie lived pretty damn well here on The King's Land.

I pulled open the wide door and the cats came out to greet me. Sally, in the corner, lifted her head, thumped her tail once, and then sighed, tucking her nose under her leg. I heard the party in the far stall and rolled my eyes.

"Bea!" I shouted and there was a sudden silence from the back. The sound of guilt.

"Guys," my sister said. "Relax. She's not, like, my mom."

"I'm the closest thing you've got." I turned the corner and found my sister in her dark blue Versace gown with the hem pulled up around her knees, sitting on top of a bale of hay, the chalkboard from the office behind her.

A bottle of bourbon was tucked between her thighs.

Of course. Of-fucking-course.

The stall next door was full of a mare in the first stages of giving birth. Oscar, Tony, and a bunch of the other guys were milling between the two stalls.

My sister looked like me but scaled to a different size. She was small. Short and slight. Her eyes—and her attitude—were the biggest things about her.

Bea was eighty percent attitude, ten percent eyes, and the rest of her was fun.

The combination was catnip for a certain kind of man.

The dress she wore made her catnip to the rest of them.

"Bea." I propped my hand against the doorway. "What are you doing?"

"Well, Cosmic is having a baby." Bea pointed over the stall. "And I'm just taking a few bets."

This shouldn't be a surprise. Drinking bourbon during my engagement party and playing bookie was completely par for Bea's course.

"Has the party started?" she asked and took a swig of bourbon. The hay was stuck all over her dress and her super-expensive shoes with the red soles had been kicked into the corner.

"Yeah," I said.

"Oops." Bea winced and hopped off the hay bale. Once we were face-to-face she only came up to my shoulders, but she hugged me, smiling at me all the while.

"You look hot, sis," she said.

"Thanks, Bea." It was impossible to stay mad at her. My sister sparkled like midnight. Like the fun and possibility of a night, just as it was getting interesting.

She turned to Oscar and Tony. "No playing with the board. If that baby is a boy and born before midnight you owe me a shit ton of money."

The guys laughed and she handed Tony her bottle of bourbon so she could put on her shoes and stand another three inches taller.

"Let's go celebrate." She smelled like hay and horse, bourbon and perfume. Eau de Bea. "Pretty necklace," she said, smiling at me.

"You think?" I put my palm over it.

"*You* think, and that's all that matters." Bea pulled us to a stop just outside the back door. "You deserve this."

"A big awful party?"

"A big beautiful man. A big beautiful love."

My chest felt too small to hold my heart. "It's going to be all right, isn't it?"

My sister—dangerous, impetuous, and reckless, but also wise—cupped my face in her hands. "Better than all right," she said. "It's going to be perfect."

We walked back into the kitchen and down the hallway to the sounds of the party. We turned a corner and nearly ran into Jennifer.

"There you are." Jennifer's smile barely made a dent in her face. "Veronica, your father would like to see you in his study."

"How about me?" Bea asked, sarcastic and smiling. "What should I do?"

"Clean yourself up and try not to embarrass your father."

Bea wrinkled her nose. "Boring. I'll go with Ronnie."

We plucked the last two glasses of champagne from a waiter's tray and turned left down the hallway, away from the party, to my father's study. The door was on the other end of the hallway, and Bea and I were sipping our drinks and whispering about Jennifer's Botox addiction, but still we were able to hear Clayton's voice.

"That was the deal, Hank," he said.

He sounded mad and I picked up my pace. Clayton rarely got angry, but when he did, it took him a while to cool off and I didn't want him angry tonight. I wanted him smiling. His hand on the small of my back. His breath against my skin as he leaned down to whisper in my ear.

"I'm marrying your daughter. I'm securing your assets for another generation, if not more. We signed a contract!"

Bea and I shared one shocked look and then I pick up the pace, spilling champagne everywhere as I practically ran down the hallway.

"You are clearly trying to renegotiate the baby bonus." Dad's laugh was familiar. Satisfied. The laugh he laughed when he had all the power and didn't mind using it.

We got to the doorway of the study just as Clayton grabbed my father by the lapels of his tux.

"You wanted her married. I'm doing that. That was the deal. Now give me the deed to the goddamned land!" Clayton shouted.

The champagne glass fell from my suddenly numb fingers and found the small slice of wood between the carpeted hallway and the Oriental rug on the floor of father's study.

It shattered spectacularly.

I felt Bea behind me. Could sort of tell she was trying to hold me up. Or back. Hard to say.

The world was moving so fast. Too fast.

"What's happening?" I whispered.

If I'd had doubts about what was happening—if I'd

thought I could find one shred of hope to cling to—that vanished when I saw Clayton's face.

The guilt was all over his cruel, handsome features. In the dark pools of his eyes. His rude-boy lips were a straight ugly line.

"What are you doing here?" he asked.

"What are *you* doing here?" Bea demanded, but Clayton didn't even blink.

"You should go back out to the party," he said to me. Like I was a child. Or a pet he could send away.

"Tell me what's happening. Tell me about...your deal," I said.

"Veronica." My father sat down behind his desk, looking far too pleased with himself. He twisted his pinky ring around his finger. "You can't be this naïve."

"What is he talking about?" Bea asked, grabbing my hand.

"He's marrying you for money," Dad said. "Specifically, my money. By way of my company. Oh, stop, Veronica. Don't look so damn hurt. I have to protect King Industries, and the best way I can do that is get someone I trust in the family. You have your charms, but you didn't think Clayton was suddenly interested in my plain, dull daughter. He didn't choose you—"

"Stop!" Clayton snapped. "Not another word."

My dad shut up, but the words were out.

Plain and *dull* didn't even hurt. The rest of it, though...

He didn't choose you.

"This is when you tell me it's not what it seems," I said to Clayton. Practically begging him to pull the wool back over my eyes. "Or...there's an explanation. That this isn't true."

Clayton was silent.

"Say something!" I yelled.

"It's true."

I put my hand against my stomach and looked down at the pretty confection of a dress, expecting blood. Rivers of it. Because surely he'd killed me.

"Veronica," Clayton said, and when I looked at him he'd pulled himself together and it was Clayton Rorick, impervious and distant, looking back at me.

Cold. So damn cold.

Had I dreamed he cared?

That he loved me?

Stupid, Veronica. You really are so stupid.

What made sense between a man like him and a woman like me? That he would feel something for my above-average wit and my below-average body?

Or that my father was paying him to marry me?

"The arrangement I have with your father has nothing to do with us," Clayton said.

I opened my mouth to laugh. I really thought I was going to laugh. Because I wanted to be that woman who could laugh at the man who'd just ripped out her heart, but it came out a sob.

I swallowed it. "What, exactly, is the arrangement between you and my father?"

"I don't think—"

"Tell me!" I shrieked, going full banshee on him.

"Upon our engagement and the securing of his property to the King bloodline, he will give me some property I have been trying to buy from him for a number of years."

"Securing?"

"A baby," my sister spat, and my heart shattered.

Clayton stepped forward like he might touch me, and I jerked back so hard I bashed into the doorjamb and sparks of pain filled my head. My knees buckled.

"Veronica!" He rushed toward me. "Are you all right?"

Thank God for Bea. My sister pulled me into her arms and put a hand out to stop Clayton.

"No!" she yelled. Unbelievably he listened and just stood there, a foot from me, strong and gorgeous and...evil. So damn evil.

Remember this. Remember this man didn't choose you.

"The engagement is over," I said.

"Now, Ronnie." My father stood up. "You walk away from this and you're walking away from King Industries. You'll never own this company."

"I don't give a shit about your company."

"But you do give a shit about that foundation."

For a second, I wavered. Because the foundation was my mother's legacy. My legacy.

Could I just...walk away from that? From all my plans? From the future I'd worked so hard for?

Bea put her arm around me. "Don't listen to him. Don't listen to any of them. Mom would want you to have more than this."

She was right. Of course she was right.

"Get me out of here, Bea," I whispered, feeling like I might pass out. Wishing that I could.

And my sister did. She put me in her car and drove me far, far away from The King's Land.

From my engagement party.

From my fiancé, who didn't even try and stop me.

From the life that was never meant for me.

I should have known better.

BUY NOW

www.ingramcontent.com/pod-product-compliance
Lightning Source LLC
Chambersburg PA
CBHW071514140726
47997CB00005B/1965